KISS AND KILL, 2

Jason's Revenge

WAYNE ELLIOTT

Order this book online at www.trafford.com
or email orders@trafford.com

Most Trafford titles are also available at major online book retailers.

Printed in the United States of America.

ISBN: 978-1-4907-3061-5 (sc)
ISBN: 978-1-4907-3062-2 (e)

Trafford rev. 03/10/2014

 www.trafford.com

North America & international
toll-free: 1 888 232 4444 (USA & Canada)
fax: 812 355 4082

Chapter 1

I t was a Tuesday night, and as usual, business was slow, so after the two men settled their account, I decided to close the joint and give my employees an early night. Martha my cook, Cindy the waitress, and Joe the bartender were my trustworthy employees who had been with me from the inception of The Silver Dollar Inn. Some eleven years ago.

After all the good nights were said and the doors and windows were double-checked I made one for the road, and the grimace on my face was a sure sign that there was too much vodka and too little OJ. But the second attempt put a warm smile on my face.

A starry Bahamian sky greeted me when I exited the Silver Dollar and padlocked the front door before climbing inside Old Faithful, my '69 Dodge Charger, and made my way to Forster St. Chippingham where a warm bed awaited me.

The telephone started to ring when I opened the front door. Picking up the receiver I said in a mild tone of voice, "Hello."

"Hi darling," a lovely voice said from the other end of the line. "Miss me?"

It was the voice I was hoping to hear, and quickly replied, "Yes doll, I miss you very much, and wish you were here. By the way how are your sister and that lovely niece of yours?"

"My niece Linda is doing fine—but Kathy is not doing so well. She has nightmares from the treatment she had received from Jason's goons while they held us captive. You remember how they raped her. May they burn in hell for what they did to her. The doctor said that he believes a change in scenery may help her forget the pain."

"Sorry to hear that she is still troubled by the past, and I hope the change of scenery works."

I detected the sadness in Joyce's voice and it caused cold chills to race up and down my spine. So I felt a punch line was needed at this time so I asked, "When are you coming to lay that sweet potato pie on me, doll?"

"Ha ha ha ha." Joyce's laughter was rich as she went on to say, "Give me until Friday. That's when my cousin Florence would have flown in from North Miami Beach to take Kathy and Linda home with her."

"Okay, doll, I believe I could hold out until then."

Joyce's girlish laughter had warmed the chills in my spine and took away some of the anger I had pent up in my heart for Jason Wright. But nevertheless I cursed myself for not ending the sucker's life like I did with most of his foot soldiers. But I knew for sure one day when he got out of prison he would cross my gun sight, and I would not hesitate to take him out and send him to Satan.

My mind put Jason on the back burner when Joyce whispered in a sexy undertone, "Remember, on Friday, darling, you will get all the pie you need and a little more to be sure your appetite is satisfied."

"Okay, doll, see you on Friday and give Kathy and Linda my love."

After replacing the phone on the cradle, I polished off the rest of the screwdriver before hitting the shower.

The cold water relieved the pressure I had received from Joyce's conversation.

The bed was inviting and I drifted off to sleep. I must have gotten about a half hour of shut-eye before the disturbing instrument woke me as it cried out for attention.

I checked the clock on the northern wall, which showed 2:30 a.m., before picking up the phone.

"Yes," I said into the mouthpiece as my head started to clear.

"Yes my ass. You better get down to your club—fast," the male voice said.

"Cut the crap, and tell me what's going on," I said, still half asleep, and did not comprehend what he was talking about.

"Your worst nightmare, Willie Jackson. Now go to hell while your establishment burns to the ground."

I still didn't know what to make of the call, but I was fully awake now. So I asked him his name in hopes that he might give me a hint to his identity.

No luck. Instead he shot back, "Screw yourself, ol' man, while the Silver Dollar crumbles in the hot flames of destruction by my handiwork."

"If this is true, punk, I'll track you down, pluck your damn eyes out, and stuff them down your fuckin' throat, savvy?"

"Mr. Jackson, you got me shaking in my little boots. Now go screw yourself, sucker, while I watch the fire do its thing down here on Market Street. By the way the roof just caved in, and, I hear sirens coming. Sorry gat to split now."

"Okay, you excuse for a human being. I am on my way."

"Before you hang up, how is Joyce doing?"

"That's none of your fuckin' business, you shitless wonder, and remember this: hell's gates will not protect you from me."

"Okay, Willie, nice speech but tell your lady the stranger said hello, ha ha ha ha ha."

I heard a clap of thunder in the southern section of the sky as I hurriedly got dressed. While the caller's mocking laughter was still sounding in my ears.

The moon I had seen earlier was now hidden behind a patch of rain clouds at the center of the darkened sky. As I climbed inside the Charger and put the .38 Smith and Wesson revolver in the glove compartment before starting the engine and reversing onto Forster Street.

Two yards up from my residence, a dog began to bark. I guess from time to time most life forces will have problems in their lives. Mine at this time would depend on what greeted me when I arrived at the end of my journey.

I didn't remember speeding, but somehow I reached the Silver Dollar in record time. And after I got out of the Charger, I looked at the southern sky and could have sworn that when the moon peeped through the dark clouds, it frowned down at me as I scratched my head in disbelief.

Chapter 2

The telephone call which I had received from the person unknown, as I had guessed, was a hoax. The Silver Dollar seemed to welcome me with a smile in some unexplainable way. But to my relief, the trash tin which was outside my southern fence was the only thing with fire coming out of it.

My attention left the tin and settled on the woman who was standing in front of her house staring at the flames, while at her right foot stood a white plastic bucket.

"Good morning," I said as I went over and stood next to her. I always had a problem of saying good morning while the hour of darkness was in play. But I guess that's the way the world turns.

"Have any idea how the fire got started? By the way, my name is Jackson, Willie Jackson, and I own the Silver Dollar. And what may your name be, angel?"

"Rita Simmons and I haven't a clue, but my son Dudley may be of some help," she replied after shaking my outstretched right hand. Then went on to say, "It was he who informed me about the fire."

Rita was much younger than me, with a pretty face. Her black hair was groomed backwards and rested on her shoulder. The white cotton dress she was wearing fitted her neatly and showed all the curves on her slender body were in the right places.

I liked the way her medium-sized breasts stood firm on her chest, as a welcoming sight that completed her gorgeous package. She sure would have filled the prescription if I was in need for a female companion in my life.

A smile parted her lips as if sensing my thoughts before she called out for her son, who appeared beside me in a flash. Dudley was slim built with a handsome face, and wearing a yellow polo shirt and blue short pants.

"Yes, Mum," he said, looking a bit shy.

"Tell Mr Jackson what you know about the trash tin fire."

Dudley pulled his left thumb from his mouth, and went on to say,

"A black car with tinted windows stopped by the trash tin, then sped off. A couple seconds later it caught on fire."

"Thanks, Dudley, now was this the first time you see that car in this area?"

"Maybe, but I can't be sure."

Dudley paused for a while, then went on to say, "Two nights ago that same car was parked by the trash tin and a man and a woman who came from the club got in with some drinks in their hands and drove off."

"You did very well, Dudley," I told him, and gave him a twenty-dollar bill. A broad smile lit his round face as he said, "Thank you, sir," then passed the bill to his mother.

After accepting the money from her son Rita said, "Go bathe off now, Dudley, remember it's a school day."

"Okay, Mummy," he replied, hitting a sad note.

"Okay when the movie is finished, then you may take your bath."

"Thanks, Mum," Dudley replied gleefully as he closed the door behind him.

After Dudley departed, I turned my attention to the half-filled bucket of water and inquired, "Did you try to put out the fire, Rita?"

"Yes, but the water was like adding more fuel to it when I threw some inside the tin."

"My guess is that it was some kind of chemical compound he used to start the fire. Lend me your bucket; maybe some sand would do the trick."

"Be my guest."

A few buckets of sand and the fire was out. Someone had sent me a fiery message and I was going to rewrite the chapters in their playbook. I returned the bucket and invited Rita for cocktails on Saturday, but she took a rain check on the offer.

Chapter 3

I returned home after being satisfied that all was in order at the Silver Dollar and picked up the phone. After the third ring a sleepy voice said: "This better be good, or there's hell to pay."

"Cool it, friend, don't blow your top, I apologize for calling at this ungodly hour but I have something to lay on you that couldn't wait."

"Apology accepted but hold the line." Johnson climbed out of bed with the cordless phone and went into the front room so he didn't disturb Mrs. Johnson. "Okay Willie, shoot. You now have my undivided attention."

After bringing Johnson up to date he went on to say, "Hell, Willie, some shithead is messing with your mind. Hold the line a second; I'm switching to the next line to call the Market Street Police Station." It seemed like a long time had passed, and then Johnson was back saying, "We can't take any chances with pranks like that. There will be a CID car checking the area while foot patrol will take place by officers from the Market Street station on the hour until day breaks."

"Thanks a million, friend, I knew I could count on you for assistance. Now go back to sleep, old man, and we'll link up later."

"You bet, but I hope I could return to that dream I was having."

"What dream?" I asked and waited patiently for the story.

"I was on a deserted island with young ladies in short grass skirts fetching me my heart's desires. Now you figure out the rest."

"Ha ha, you better don't let Mrs. Johnson invade that dream, because your ass will be grass and she will be the lawn mower!"

The lukewarm bath was refreshing, and it helped me relax as I lay down in my pyjamas staring at the white ceiling, and took a tour back into time to see if I could remember someone who might be responsible for the prank, and Jason Wright was the only conclusion I could arrive at. Knowing he had the wealth and people on the outside to do his dirty work, he became my prime suspect. Especially after the person asked about Joyce.

However, I put Jason out of the equation for the time being and I turned the blame on someone who was afraid of competition from the Silver Dollar. Because I had received lots of new customers from near and far. With the latter thoughts on my mind, I closed my eyes hoping for sleep to come quickly, but the damn telephone on the nightstand forced my eyes back open.

"Yes," I barked into the disturbing instrument.

"Yes! My black ass," the caller shot back. "How was the trip and what did you find at the Silver Dollar? Is that piece of mortar and blocks still standing?"

It was the voice from the other night so I replied, "Why don't you buy a dildo and go screw yourself, punk? I don't play foolish games."

"Call it what you may, but the next time it will not be the garbage. Ha Ha Ha Ha."

My blood began to boil after the son of a bitch slammed down his phone, setting my nerves on edge. I took deep breaths and exhaled slowly to calm myself. Eventually I drifted off to dreamland and found myself in a lion's den with two half-starved critters advancing towards me after sensing I was their evening meal. But just as they pranced for the kill my telephone rang and I woke up in a cold sweat. Shit! I thought I was a goner for sure.

"Hello," I said, my voice merely a whisper.

"Sorry to wake you, darling, but I dreamt you were in some kind of danger, so I called to make sure you were all right."

"You just saved me from being eaten by two half-starved lions, Joyce, I was having a nightmare, thanks for the call."

"Glad to be of help, darling, even if only to save you from a nightmarish dream."

"You sure did, doll. Those suckers had made their move to eat me just before your call."

"Okay, darling, hope you can sleep now minus any more nightmares."

"Thanks again, love doll, see you Friday."

"You bet, Willie, I am missing you like crazy, bye for now."

"Bye."

Sleep came easy after Joyce hung up and I made it through to sunrise without any bad dreams or disturbing calls from that punk who had entered my world with the wrong acceptance speech. He was a slimeball on borrowed time, and he didn't know it yet.

Chapter 4

T he sun was midway in the clear blue sky as I climbed into the Charger and made my way to the Silver Dollar. Sergeant Johnson was seated at a table near the kitchen.

There was a small crowd and the cash register was taking in its share while the jukebox lit the atmosphere with Otis Redding singing "These Arms of Mine."

"Hello, Johnson," I said, before waving Joe over. Johnson gave me one of his big welcoming smiles as he raised his half-filled glass with rum and Coke in a salute. I made a half bow, before sitting down as Joe made his way over to the table.

"Open a tab for me and put that drink and whatever the Sergeant gets on it, Joe, now bring me a green crème de menthe with brandy and tell Martha to bring us two bowls of conch salad and to go easy on the hot pepper for mine."

"Do you want another drink now, Serge?" Joe inquired before going to the bar for my stinger.

"Yes," Johnson said as he polished off the remainder of his drink, and Joe took the empty glass with him.

The stinger was to my liking. Joe really knows his stuff. Johnson took a sip from his fresh glass before he asked, "What do you think of this puzzle, Willie?"

"Beats the shit out of me, I wanted to rest the blame at Jason Wright's but after coming and meeting the building intact, I took another direction and chalked it up to someone who feels that I am taking away from their profit line and wanted to scare me and hope that I close up shop and scamper with my tail between my legs."

"Did anyone try to buy you out at any time, Willie, or show any hostility in any way or form within the past year?"

"Not that I can remember . . . wait . . . hold on a minute. John Black from Market and Brougham Street had dropped in a few times scouting the joint, and one time, he jokingly asked me to name my price and he'll take the Silver Dollar off my hands, but we laughed it off and I never gave it a second thought until now."

"Okay, that's a place to start, Willie. I'll pay him a visit discreetly like. It may be a waste of time, but who knows we may hit pay dirt."

"Anything to get to the bottom of this mess, Johnson."

"Okay Willie, but I have something else to lay on you."

"I am all ears, buddy, shoot from the hips."

"I did some digging pertaining to those calls you had received and I was told that the first call was made from a pay phone down East Street South, in the area of Sapodilla Boulevard, but the last call came from a phone booth on South Beach Boulevard. By the way does John Black live in the south?"

"I don't know."

"Okay Willie, until further notice I'm going to put a shadow in this place. To see if we can get lucky and nail the son o' bitch. But, maybe, this joker only meant to ruffle your feathers a bit and when he's had enough he'll blow away like the summer breeze, dig?"

"Well he is doing a damn good job, Johnson, and I hope you are right. I don't need the fuckin' aggravation."

"Okay I'm going to feed the story to Inspector McClain, he's a good soldier; we fought many battles together and we are still here to joke about them."

"Okay I'll bring my staff up to date."

"No, only you and I must know about the shadow for the time being . . ." Johnson paused as he fished a photo from his inner jacket pocket and passed it to me. I took a good look and passed it back to him.

"His name is Corporal Phillips. He's been tested and passed with flying colors—he knows most of the tricks in the book."

Corporal Phillips was a slim built, dark brown, handsome chap in his late twenties. Johnson left the club and I got up and made a beeline to the jukebox. After punching my first record, a female voice behind me asked: "May I have a record please?"

"Yes you may," I said and slightly turned to see who the lovely voice had belonged to. As her soft body brushed up to me to gain access to punch her record, I caught a whiff of her expensive perfume.

"Thank you, sir," the lady with the lavender blouse, black pants, and black shoes said as she punched "P.14" and went back to her seat at the bar.

"I've Got Dreams to Remember," a second song sung by Otis Redding, filled the club's atmosphere as the loud talking quieted down to a mere whisper to listen to Otis do his number.

The lady who had bummed the record was a beauty and looked a bit younger than Joyce. On a scale from one to ten, she was eight and a half. My love doll had her by a point. I would have gladly taken her to the crib for drinks and romance if I was cruising the joint for pickups.

The stingers were starting to creep up on me so I decided to head for home. I waved Joe over and paid the tab for the drinks and salads.

Otis had finished his tune and "Sexual Healing" by Marvin Gay came on. It was the one I had pushed so I got up to leave as visions of my love doll's beautiful face filled my brain waves and the lust for her sexy body sent a warm feeling to my groin.

I made my way through the side door and got inside the Charger to my surprise, an uninvited guest eased herself into the passenger seat saying, "May I bum a ride? By the way my name is Elizabeth Culmer and thanks again for the record."

"I am heading in the direction of Chippingham, by the way, my name is Jackson, Willie Jackson."

"We are going to South Beach, Mr. Jackson," she said in a harsh tone of voice after sticking a .22 revolver in my side, which came from her black pocketbook.

"Any objections?"

"No, but why the peashooter, Miss Culmer? If you would have given me your directions, I would have been more than happy to make the detour."

"It's a little persuasive tool, I never leave home without it. Now cut the crap and let's go, at this range this little fellow could do as much damage as a .38 revolver so don't fuck with me, Mr. Jackson."

Chapter 5

I drove west along John Street to Blue Hill Road, then made a left turn and continued in a southwardly direction. As the Charger rolled on I thought about starting a conversation but quickly changed my mind. I concluded that it would be fruitless and I didn't want to make matters worse.

The world outside the confinement of my automobile didn't seem to exist until I got a glimpse of the blue waters of South Beach as we came to the T-junction where South Beach Boulevard connected with Baillou Hill Road.

"Make a left here," Elizabeth ordered as she poked my side with the firearm which kept me at bay.

After driving about one hundred feet along South Beach Boulevard, I got my second command.

"Take a left at the phone booth and drive with caution. Because the road will be bumpy in some spots and this gun might accidentally go off."

I heeded the warning and drove with caution along the narrow dirt road which opened up to a paved parking lot with several parked cars outside a white building trimmed black.

There was a sign on the door which read "The Pussy Cat Lair," and it was spelled in golden letters, while standing majestically on both sides of the entrance were two large marble cats, one painted white and the other black.

I was surprised when I entered the building and saw it was a restaurant and bar. It didn't say so on the entrance door, but my gut feelings told me it was a member's only establishment.

There was a small crowd in the place enjoying themselves until Elizabeth and I entered the joint. Everyone stopped what they were doing and I became the center of attraction.

After a few seconds the excitement was over and it was business as usual. The jukebox was punched and James Brown's voice filled the club's atmosphere singing "Please Don't Go."

The lady with the neat afro stopped her laughter when she saw the muscle-bound ape came from behind the bar and made a beeline towards Elizabeth and me. As the slim man got up from her table and went to the jukebox, his face looked familiar but I couldn't place it. My guess was that he was going to play a love tune for his chick with the afro and the complexion of brown sugar. Ten give you twenty my odds were she was sweeter than the sugar.

"Who's the pretty boy, Liz, is he the one getting all my honey?"

"Cool it, Chris, you know it isn't anything between us, but for your satisfaction the boss wants to see him, like as of yesterday."

"Oh!" Chris exclaimed and stepped aside.

I gave Chris the index finger before going through a door which led into a hallway with three other doors. One was marked "Boss" and the other two were ladies and gents restrooms.

Elizabeth rapped on the "Boss's" door and a male voice growled,

"Come in."

When we entered the room, the bald-headed man who had called us in was sitting on his mahogany desk with his back towards the door getting a blow job from a young woman who seemed to be in her early twenties, while a second one sucked on his left nipple as he fingered her vagina. Through his pleasure, he managed to ask, "Who is it?"

"Elizabeth, sir, and I brought Mr. Jackson as you instructed."

"Ooooh! Yessss!" he screamed as he released himself.

After the young women left, he took a seat behind his desk and lit a cigar before pressing a button under the desk. Both Elizabeth and I were taken aback when the door suddenly opened and Chris and a second ape entered the room.

"You may leave now, Elizabeth. Go behind the bar and retrieve the envelope with your name, and, I don't want to see you in these parts again. Do I make myself clear?"

"Like crystal, sir."

"So we meet again, Jackson, but this time you don't have a nurse maid watching your fucking back."

Prince Brown had not changed. The years had done nothing to his ugly mug, and he still reeked of cheap cigars. Hell by now I'd figured he should have moved up to the expensive kind like the ones from Havana. But I guess a cheap hood will always be a cheap son o' bitch.

"Get a good grip on that motherfucker," Prince ordered. "It's payback time." Those apes held me so firm, I felt like I was in a human vice grip.

"Take your best shot, you . . . ." I could not finish the sentence. Prince landed a haymaker in my midsection, then he landed one that made my right jaw, causing it to go numb.

"That one is for Mr. Wright and this is for the time in your house," Prince said as he sent a punch back to my midsection and the next to my left jaw. I felt like a couple of teeth got shaken from that blow. Then a right uppercut sent me down for the count.

"Take this piece of shit out of my sight and throw some water on him. When he comes to tell him Mr. Wright sends his regards until they meet again."

The two apes threw a bucket of water over me and delivered the message along with a couple of kicks to my side for good measure. Before throwing me outside. I heard their laughter in the distance as I hobbled to my vehicle and fished the keys from my pocket. The engine started with one turn so I beat a hasty retreat from the Pussy Cat Lair's parking lot, battered and bruised but in one piece.

Chapter 6

My body ached all over as I made it towards South Beach Boulevard from the dirt road. With my thoughts all in a mess, I fought off dizzy spells that came over me, but, as a silent prayer escaped my lips, a renewed energy surged throughout my body and left me fully alert. I believed my prayers were answered.

I made a left turn on the boulevard and headed for East Street. I wanted to take the quickest way back to safety and put the beating Prince and his goons put on me to the back of my mind until it was time to make them all pay for the mistake they'd made by not sending me to the morgue.

While I was checking the damage they had done to my face in the rear-view mirror, I saw a white car exit the dirt road from the Pussy Cat's Lair. At the time it didn't arouse my suspicion, but my thinking quickly changed when the car got in full view and I made out the driver to be Chris and the other ape who'd dumped me outside.

I floored the gas pedal and watched the speed needle climb from 25 to 55 and settle at 70 MPH as I outdistanced the Sedan, but quickly reduced my speed just in time to avoid hitting a Chevy SS that carelessly pulled out of Johnson Drive in front of me. Due to the idiot's stupidity when I swung out from him, I caused a black truck heading in the opposite direction to run off the road.

After clearing the hurdle, I found myself with a larger distance on the white Ford as I turned left on to East Street.

Luck was on my side: I did not see any sign of Chris and his punk friend. Until I passed a sign which read No

Dumping: then I saw Chris turn onto East Street and come burning up the asphalt in his quest to catch me.

A smile toyed on my puffed lip as I saw the police cruiser heading in our direction; ever so quickly the Charger was down to 15 MPH. I tooted my horn as the two officers went by. Unfortunately for Prince Brown's bloodhounds, they were pulled over by the approaching officer.

By the time I reached Market Street and Wulff Road, I had decided not to return to the Silver Dollar in my condition and made my way to Chippingham.

The pain had subsided a bit and most of the swelling had gone down. I dialled Sgt. Johnson's work number after swallowing two pain killers.

"Sergeant Johnson here, how may I help you?"

"I want to report an abduction and assault, Sergeant," I replied.

"Is Joyce alright, Willie?"

"She is fine."

"Then who was taken and assaulted?"

"Me."

"Cut the crap, Willie," Johnson said jokingly. As he knew from time to time I would tickle his funny bone.

"I'm serious this time, friend, come over to the house and bring a doctor you can trust. I'm keeping this on the down low."

Half an hour later a loud rapping sounded on the front door.

"It's open, Johnson," I said and pulled myself to a sitting position in the settee after hiding my revolver under the middle cushion.

Johnson was followed by a slim light-skinned man carrying a small black bag like the ones doctors carry.

"Damn Willie, you look like shit," Johnson said. "Your eye is puffy with a red spot and your jaw is a bit swollen."

"Thanks, I feel like shit too," I replied and forced a grin, which hurt like hell. "Who's the guy with the black bag?"

"Doctor Simmons," Johnson replied, "and he will have you fit as a fiddle in no time."

"Hello, Mr. Jackson," Doctor Simmons said as he rested down his bag.

"Only to strangers, Doc, you are a friend now so you may call me Willie."

Doc's handsome face broke into a smile as he pulled his stethoscope from the black bag and went to work. With the exception of some swelling and body aches, Doc gave me a good bill of health along with an injection, some tablets, and a small tube of eye ointment.

"What's my damage, Doc?"

"We'll chalk it up to friendship now, if you have some cold brew I'll drink a couple before I leave, but I want you to take some rest, Willie."

"You are my kind of man, Doc, go to the fridge and help yourself."

After Doctor Simmons left, I brought Johnson up to date on what had taken place at the Pussy Cat's Lair.

A sad look came over his face when he said, "I should have stayed a bit longer, Willie, maybe none of this would have happened."

"Don't blame yourself, friend, this incident may have been written many years ago somewhere in the wide blue yonder, and like they say you never pass nothing until you're six feet under."

"Okay, but I'm going to stop it from occurring again if it is in my power now. Give me the directions to the Lair.

21

This is the first time I'm hearing that damn name, Willie. They must be operating under the radar. Pussy Cat Lair, I wonder what else goes on in there?"

"Not now, Johnson, when you make that move I want to be well enough to accompany you so I can teach those sons of bitches a lesson in respect, dig?"

"As you wish, Willie. By the way, the shadow is in place. Hopefully we may get a lead on that punk who was making those calls, and put an end to this bunch of crap."

"That's welcoming news to my sore ears, Johnson, thanks for the power boost, buddy. Now I can rest well knowing your man is on the job."

Johnson left and I picked up the phone to call Joyce, but after second thoughts, I decided not to put the extra stress on her since her hands were already full with her sister's problem.

I had to forgo my bath. The medication Doc gave me sent me into the world where make-believe becomes reality.

The sleep had done wonders for me. The swelling, pain, and red eye were now a bad memory. I climbed into the lukewarm water and felt renewed after my bath and swore that Prince Brown and the others would feel my wrath whenever the opportunity presented itself; I hoped it'd be sooner rather than later.

Just as I was about to vacate the tub, the telephone rang. I dried off in quick time and caught it on the fourth ring.

The voice at the end of the line was sweet music to my ear. It sounded soft and mellow, but it lost its caressing appeal when Joyce said, "My darling, I had another bad dream about you last night . . ." Joyce paused, then went on to say, "I dreamt that you were killed by Jason Wright when you entered his mansion."

"Dreams don't always come true, love doll. You know I can take anything Jason throws at me. Have no fear, you and I are going to be around until the big man in the sky calls us home, so don't worry your pretty head about that rodent. I will catch him in my trap and deal with him accordingly."

"Okay, Willie, I'll do my best. See you on Friday, my love, but please be careful."

"For your sake, love doll, I'll be extra careful."

"Bye, Willie."

"Bye, love doll."

Chapter 7

In today's world where medical science had advanced, I guess anything was possible with the right financial backing and friends in the right places. One could sometimes get away with almost anything. And it was to me no different in Jason's case.

Some time ago I along with Sam Prince and Sgt Johnson put Jason Wright away for aiding and abetting in the abduction of Joyce and her sister Kathy and for stockpiling unlicensed weapons at his mansion. But a psychiatrist persuaded the court that Jason was sick in his mind and needed treatment in a mental institute instead of a jail cell.

Now a few years later, Jason's case came up for review and that same psychiatrist told the board that Jason had somehow miraculously pulled out of his dilemma and can be placed behind bars with less stressful encounters because he was ready to atone for his wrongdoing to the society at large. Whatever the hell that means. But to me it said that he had greased the right palms and now the wheels were spinning in his favor. The finger was pointed at me and Sam Prince, indicating that we took the law in our own hands when we went to Jason's mansion to free Joyce and Kathy.

But when the roof was about to come crashing down, Sgt. Johnson came to the rescue saying we deserved a medal for the good deed we had done. After putting our lives on the line to help out the two ladies who were held captive and used as sex toys by Jason and his goons.

The roof held firm, and we were sent on our merry way with a stiff warning to let the law deal with criminal matters. That's why Sam married Brenda and moved to Ft. Lauderdale, Florida, his wife's native land.

The first ring from my telephone went unnoticed because I must have dozed off. I got it on the third ring. It was Joe the bartender.

"Good afternoon, sir, we are running low on supplies for the bar and kitchen," Joe said in a mild tone of voice.

"Have you drawn up a list yet?" I asked in a self-satisfying way, because I was proud to have such attentive people on the payroll.

"Yes, sir."

"Okay, put Martha on the line."

"Hello, boss," Martha's pleasant voice said when she came on the line.

"Hello, Martha, call the suppliers and place the orders C.O.D."

"Okay, boss, will do."

I felt contented with my staff; they are always on time, they know what was expected of them, and they deliver one hundred and ten percent. And if I couldn't be reached Martha would have ordered the stuff and filled me in later.

I was feeling hungry and the stomach worms were getting restless. The leftover fried chicken and white rice went down nicely with the Coke soda.

My worms were satisfied with the intake so I turned the tube on for some relaxation and caught one of my favorite movies, *Combat*, starring Vic Morrow and Rick Jason. War and western movies were two of my favorite pastimes. I always figure the romantic movies were more for the female gender, but I do like the lovemaking scenes when I'm watching one with Joyce. They were her favorites.

The medication and rest had worked wonders for me, so I climbed into a pair of jeans and a dirty old man tee shirt and had a little trouble deciding which tennis shoes to put on from the six pairs I had, so I slipped on the black strollers instead and settled the tug-of-war in my mind.

Shit! If everything was that easy, there would be no need for war. The generals could sit down at the table stone-faced and stare each other down, then after a few minutes, figure out what caused them to be at the table in the first damn place. Then maybe a smile could turn into laughter and then a good friendly handshake would send them home happy and there would be no need to send in the tanks.

The sun had set in the west and the street lights came on. I climbed inside the Charger and made my way to my establishment.

The shadow, Corporal Phillips who was every bit of his photograph, was sitting at the bar drinking a Becks beer. I went by without a second look in his direction.

"Good to see you, boss," Martha greeted as I entered the kitchen. I could see in her eyes she had sensed something was wrong, but my warm smile made her change her mind as I went on to respond:

"Good to see you too. How are things?"

"All is in order," she replied, handing me the receipts from the purchasing she had done.

"Thank you, Martha," I said, taking them from her, and left the kitchen.

The shadow was not at the bar when I returned.

"Hello, Joe," I said as I went behind the bar and placed the receipts in the tin where I keep them until the end of the week, before taking them home to post in the ledgers.

"Hello, boss, should I fix you a stinger?"

"No, just give me a shot of brandy on the rocks."

Corporal Phillips emerged from the restroom area and gave me a slight nod indicating to meet him on the outside. But, before following him I went over to the jukebox and punched I-12 and listened a bit to Frank Sinatra's voice as he sang "Strangers in the night."

Corporal Phillips was standing in front of a red Mustang, and when he saw me exit the club, he climbed inside and drove off slowly south on Market Street.

I climbed inside the Charger and followed the Mustang at a distance until it turned into Scotia Bank parking lot. Phillips exited the vehicle and went inside to use the ATM machine. I did likewise.

"Hello, Mr. Jackson," Phillips said as we shook hands.

"Only to strangers, Corporal, to you Willie."

A smile lit Phillips' face as he went on to say, "And you may call me Sam. By the way, a couple of known hoodlums had been in the club. The first one was Carl Smith. He purchased a few items and left. The second one was Patrick Clarke. He bought a half-pint gin and tonic, stayed at the bar, and left when it was finished. Neither men showed any suspicious intentions."

"Thanks for the report, Sam. When do you go off duty?"

Sam pulled out a photo of his relief and gave it to me, saying, "This is Constable Mackey; and he's at your place now until it closes. After that a car and foot patrols will make periodic checks until the matter is closed."

"Thanks, Sam. I'll remember to send a check to the police reward-and-find fund for this year.

Corporal Samuel Phillips laughed as we shook hands before he left. He went on to inform me that Sgt. Johnson didn't have time to fill me in on Constable Mackey joining the fold.

Chapter 8

There were talks in the air that the PLM party, which had lost most of its moneymen and some supports after the stink with Jason Wright, had regrouped and was gaining momentum, and word on the street was they stood a good damn chance of becoming the next government.

Today was Friday and my love doll was coming home. Somehow I felt like I could take on the world. But before I tried the impossible, I would give her a proposal I hoped she couldn't refuse.

The front door opened and my ray of sunshine entered the house. Joyce was even lovelier than before in her red dress.

"Hello, darling," she said with a smile as broad as Andros. "I'm back."

I took her in my arms and said, "Good to have you back."

After carrying Joyce into the bedroom, our garments hit the floor in record time and the pent-up passion exploded into a joyful bliss as Joyce began to moan and groan as we, slowly, crossed the ageless boundaries of ecstasy and eased into a wonderland of sexual fulfilment. As she sung her praise.

"Oooooh God damn, Willie, that was fantastic. Maybe I should visit my aunty in Acklins Island for a few days, if the return home will be so sexually rewarding."

"Amen!" I exclaimed and rolled off Joyce saying, "Tomorrow I will fill you in on the latest."

"Okay, Willie, good night."

As I travelled in the dimly lit world of make-believe I saw myself walking through a cornfield when gunshots rang out behind me, followed by Jason shouting, "You can't run from me, Jackson! My men are going to catch you and cut your balls off and give them to your whore, Joyce." After Jason finished spewing his bullshit, he and his men sent more bullets in my direction.

"Ouch," I heard myself cry out in pain as a shell grazed my left shoulder, which stung like hell.

"Ha ha!" Jason laughed out loud. "I winged you that time, sucker, next time it will be at the center of your back."

"Go to hell, Jason!" I shouted as I ran towards a bright orange truck and where Joyce was shouting, "Come on, Willie, before those suckers kill you."

As I reached for the door, a bullet caught me in the left leg. But instead of going down, I picked up more speed and climbed inside the vehicle and my love doll drove us to safety.

It was silent as the grave the following morning when we ate breakfast.

I couldn't avoid it any longer so I told Joyce about the phone calls and the events that followed, and watched as sadness crept over her lovely face before she went on to say as she tried hard to keep her composure, "Willie I am afraid for us, darling."

"Dearest Joyce, have no fear we will come out on top," I said coaxingly.

"I believe we will, but you are alone now. Sam is no longer on the island."

Just as I was about to mention Sgt. Johnson's name, a knock sounded on the back door and Joyce jumped in her chair. "Don't answer it, darling," Joyce said as she sat tensed in her chair.

"Don't worry, doll, I have Betsy with me," I said and waved the .38 in the air, then went on to say, "This is my equalizer."

After seeing the weapon, a smile lit her face as the fear vanished.

When I opened the door, I hid the firearm because I was greeted by a smiling young boy who handed me an envelope, then said, "Mr. Jackson, a man in a black car told me to give it to you."

"Thank you, sonny," I said and fished a dollar bill from my pocket.

"No thanks, that man paid me a $20 bill to make the delivery."

I asked him to identify the man and the description he gave fitted the man to the tee whom Dudley believed had set the garbage on fire by the Silver Dollar.

The little boy left and my blood began to boil after I read the note. That sucker had stepped up his cat-and-mouse games and up the ante with a piece of paper which stated: *Judgement Day is coming soon, Willie. You and everyone dear to you will be destroyed along with the Silver Dollar.*

Before going back to Joyce, I calmed my nerves down and lied, saying, "It was nothing to worry about, doll," while stashing the note in my pocket before she could have seen it. "The neighbors' kid wanted to get some limes that dropped from the tree."

"Okay," Joyce said, picking up our dirty dishes.

"Need any help?"

"No, darling."

"Okay then, I'm going to the Silver Dollar."

"Tell the staff hello and that I'll visit them soon."

"I will, doll. See you later."

There were a few people in the establishment when I arrived, but the man dressed in all black got my full attention when I entered the building.

"Give me a gin and tonic, Joe," I said and sat at the bar while I glanced around the joint in search of the shadow and discovered that he was nowhere in sight.

"Here you are, sir, one gin and tonic," Joe said while placing the drink in front of me.

"Thanks, Joe. Now, tell me how long that guy in the black outfit has been here?"

"He's only been here about twenty minutes, sir."

"Okay, Joe. Thanks for the info, now go tell Martha and Cindy that Joyce said hello and that she will be coming to visit soon but before you go, have you ever seen that guy in here before?"

"Yes, boss, I believe he was in here last week some time, and if I'm not mistaken him and that lady was in here three weeks ago."

"You sure about that, Joe?" I asked with a bittersweet taste in my mouth to know I may have struck pay dirt.

"Bet the family jewels on it, sir, and they are my most priceless treasure."

"Thanks, Joe. Now go tell the others what Joyce had said, I'll tend the bar until you get back." When Joe left I started my calculation, and bingo that son of a bitch is the rat who pressed his luck too far. So now the trap is about to pop his fuckin' neck.

Corporal Phillips entered the club and sat on the stool I had just vacated. And proved the old saying was wrong this time because when I needed a cop one appeared.

"What can I get for you, sir?" I asked as I wrote a short note for Phillips telling him that I suspected the man sitting with the lady may have sent me this note. And I believed he was the one making those calls to my residence.

"Coke soda," Phillips replied as I slipped him both notes.

"One can of Coke coming up, sir."

Phillips finished his Coke, placed a five-dollar bill on the counter, and said, "I'll be back for the change. I have to get something from my vehicle and it won't take long."

"Okay, I'll be here with your change," I said jokingly.

Det. Cpl. Phillips returned for his change and secretly passed me a note which read, *Sgt. Johnson is parked in his vehicle awaiting a car from C.I.D. who will pick up my suspect.* Just as I put the note in my pocket two detectives walked in, stopped at the bar, and Phillips pointed to the culprit who was sitting with his lady having a gin and tonic.

"Sir," the slim, light-skinned officer said while producing his I.D. card.

"My name is Det. Const. Rolle and this is Det. Const. Pratt, and what may be your name?"

"Johnny Russell, and may I ask what is the meaning of this intrusion, and can a man have a quiet drink with his lady?"

"We apologize, sir, but you are needed at headquarters to straighten out a matter," Det. Const. Pratt chimed in.

"You can say what it is in front of my woman," Johnny said defiantly.

"Sir, we prefer to deal with the matter at H.Q.," Rolle said as his patience had worn thin.

Johnny Russell stood up and dropped a hundred-dollar bill on the table, saying, "That should hold you till I get back."

"Okay, Johnny," she said and put the hundred-dollar bill in her black purse. As Johnny went by our eyes locked and they spoke to each other. My eyes told him "Now I got you, scumbag"; his eyes replied "Not by a long shot." My eyes knew his eyes were talking horse shit.

Shortly after the officers left, Sgt. Johnson entered with a big smile on his face. It was a look of satisfaction. After doing a good deed for man and country.

"Give me a Becks, bartender," Johnson said, taking a seat on the barstool.

"You heard the man, Joe," I chimed in. After receiving his beer Johnson and I went over to Johnny's girl table.

"May we join you?" I asked.

"I believe it's your place and you could do as you please," she said with a voice loaded with hostility as she spoke.

"Oh no," Johnson said, "you are a paying customer and this is your space. What you say goes. Come, Willie, let's go back to the bar."

"In that case you both may join me until my man gets back." Seeing that it was her call to make, she sounded more pleasant this time when she spoke. I believe she felt she held power over the man who may have done her injustice.

"Why did the officer take your friend away?" Johnson asked, pretending not to know about the situation.

"He was taken to settle a matter."

"Oh!" Johnson exclaimed. "Care for a drink, lovely lady? Your glass is empty."

"No thanks."

"May I ask your name, pretty lady?" I chimed in and was looking for an insult, but got a surprise instead.

"Betty Wright and what may yours be, innkeeper?"

"My name is Willie Jackson, and how did you know I own the joint?"

"You look the part and also when you came in you sat at the bar, said something to the bartender, then took over his job as he went into the kitchen."

"You sure you are not an undercover cop?" I teased, and liked how her smile warmed her dark brown face.

"No sir, I'm not; I'm just a big girl whose boyfriend was escorted out of your establishment, for what reason I do not know." Betty's voice was soft and filled with fright.

"May I ask you a couple of questions, Miss Wright?" Johnson inquired and saw a frown come over her face when he showed her his ID card.

"I had a feeling you were C.I.D.," she said. "I have nothing to fear; go ahead ask away, but if they are too personal, I'll just clump up, dig?"

"Fine by me," Johnson said assuringly.

"This lady has beauty and brains, Johnson, be careful," I said, taking a sip of my gin and tonic.

"First of all, Miss Wright, I don't want to implicate you in anything, so keep that in mind as I ask the questions, OK?"

"OK," she replied. This time the frown had changed into a warm smile.

Chapter 9

Betty Wright listened attentively to every word that was uttered by Johnson. While trying hard to conceal any true knowledge he may have touched on. From time to time she shifted in her chair, when Johnson may have hit something on the head.

Johnson had told her about my dilemma, and informed her that her boyfriend Johnny may be involved. He even showed her the note I had gotten from someone fitting her boyfriend's description.

"Sorry to disappoint you two gentlemen, but I can't assist you in any way. Now which one of you handsome gentlemen is going to furnish that drink I was first offered?"

I signalled to Joe and he came over smiling.

"A round of drinks for the table, and put it on my tab."

"Gatcha, boss," Joe said and stopped momentarily to take an order from a customer in a light blue shirt on his way back to the bar.

"Anyone care for lunch?"

"Yes," Betty and Johnson replied.

I waved Cindy over after she had served four scorched conchs to the table across from ours.

"Yes, boss," she said as she stood with her pen ready to take our order.

"I'll take the chicken snack with lettuce and tomatoes," I told Cindy, then turned to Miss Wright and said, "The chicken snack is great."

"Okay, I'll have a breast with lots of fries," she said, then took a sip of her vodka and orange juice.

"And you, Mr. Johnson?" Cindy asked.

"I'll have the same thing Miss Wright is having."

"How long were you and Johnny an item, Miss Wright?" I asked out of curiosity.

"You may call me Betty, and it has been just over a year."

"Is he employed?"

"Not at the moment."

"So how does he keep up with the expensive duds and maintain someone as refined as you?" Johnson chimed in, and watched her blush.

"He told me he has a rich benefactor who takes care of him."

"You wouldn't know this person's name, by any chance?" I asked, hoping to hear the name Jason Wright or Prince Brown escape her lips.

"No," she replied after giving the question some consideration.

The food came and we ate. I knew before long, one of us had to tell her that her boyfriend was not returning any time soon. So I was going to leave it for Johnson to take care of.

After the table got cleaned, we had another round of drinks that Johnson insisted on picking up that tab for. After paying the bill he went on to say, "Sorry Betty, but Johnny won't be coming back for hours. You know how busy things can get at the police station. But could I offer you a lift anywhere?"

"I don't believe it was him doing those crazy things," Betty said, "but as for the ride, thanks, but I'll catch a cab."

Betty Wright paid the tab she and Johnny had made and Joe called her a cab. I was beginning to feel a bit sorry for her. She was the kind of female who gets caught up in relationships with men and don't know what the hell they were and are into. Sometimes love could be a downer.

Betty left and Johnson said, "I'm going to put the squeeze on Johnny Russell and pump him for what it's worth, Willie. And I'll get back to you later and bring you up to date."

"Okay Johnson, I'm going to catch up on some bookwork. By the way, Joyce is back and Kathy and Linda went to Florida for a while."

"I guess it's for the better," Johnson said, referring to Kathy and Linda, then he left for his date with Johnny.

I took my work to the table by the northern door and checked the cash receipts for the past three weeks, and as usual, everything was in order and up to date. A smile toyed at my lips as I told them good-bye, then went home to Joyce. The way things were mounting up, I did not want to leave my love doll alone for long periods now that she was in harm's way with Jason's minions on the loose.

Chapter 10

D own at Bank Lane as Sgt. Johnson made his way up the stairs to C.I.D. headquarters, uniformed officers were escorting prisoners to and from the courthouses. While spectators gathered under a huge shady tree to watch as their friends and loved ones were taken to court to be judged for their alleged offences.

Johnson nodded to his colleague when he entered the building and went over to Johnny, who was seated on a bench in a northern corner of the room. Johnson then took Johnny Russell in a small room with a table and two chairs. In the center of the table was a tape recorder.

"Have a seat and no bullshit," Johnson said in a frosty tone, which sent cold chills up and down Johnny's spine as he quickly sat down like an obedient child. The resistance he'd had before took a back seat, because the rumors about some crucial measures that were undertaken in C.I.D. to get information were presently on his mind. But when Johnson smiled at him, he believed it was all nonsense, so he began to relax.

Then suddenly without warning Johnson barked, "What the hell's going on, Johnny?" Then Johnson got up abruptly, pushing the chair back. The calm smiling man had turned into a raging madman.

"Now listen to this recorded voice, and tell me if it's yours or not."

Johnny's face showed fear as his heart skipped a beat, and he almost pissed his pants. Because he was afraid of what the tape might reveal.

Johnson's face was now calm as he sat back down and continued the interrogation as he went on to say, "You see, son o' bitch, we taped that last conversation, and I believe it is your voice on this tape aggravating Mr. Jackson, do you need to hear it?"

"No sir, it was me who made the calls but I was paid a couple hundred dollars to make them," Johnny confessed. "I thought it was all a prank."

"Who paid you the dough?"

"It was a bald-headed black man. No names were exchanged but he told me what to say and when to say it."

"We know you used two different pay phones. Now where were you recruited for the job?"

"It was in a hideaway club called 'The Pussycat's Lair' down in South Beach, where I was having cocktails when a muscle-bound ape approached me and asked me if I wanted to make a few hundred bucks. At the time, I couldn't refuse the offer."

"Did you light the fire in the trash tin?"

"Yes."

"So why were you in the Silver Dollar today? And do you still think this whole thing is still a fucking prank?" Johnson asked, producing the note Johnny had paid the young boy to deliver.

"It was the last part of the job, and no I don't think this matter is a prank, so I want out. Just tell me what you want me to do and it will be a pleasure to be on the right side of the law."

Johnson didn't have a mug shot of Prince Brown for Johnny to I.D. so he said, "Okay, Johnny, you're keeping bad company. Betty is a fine lady, change your ways and do right by her, because if you even cross my path again for any sort of offence, I'll throw the book at you. And by the way, who did that poor dog in?"

"Yes sir, Mr. Johnson, and thanks for the advice. I needed that. Dog, what dog? I know nothing about any dog."

Johnny reached out his right hand to Johnson, who took it. After shaking hands both men now had a smile on their faces, but as Johnny turned to leave, Johnson stopped him as he reached for the doorknob, saying, "Listen to this, Johnny." Johnny halted in his tracks and got the surprise of his life when he heard Otis Redding's voice singing, "I've Got Dreams to Remember."

"You son of a gun," Johnny said and left the room.

Night was on its way as the sun was slowly descending, in the western horizon casting its shadow on the aquamarine waters, which was an alluring sight for the visitors that flocked to the sandy beaches of the Bahamas Islands.

I was in the bathtub when Sgt. Johnson called, so he left a message with Joyce asking me to return one to him.

"What's up, Sergeant?" I asked when Johnson came on the line.

"Johnny Russell is our man," he replied.

"Okay, so where do we go from here," I inquired, feeling much relief now that I knew a part of the puzzle was solved. And I could get my just revenge on Johnny for spoiling my night rest among other things.

"Before we do anything, let's hold back for a while. I'm sending someone to do some undercover work in the Pussycat's Lair for a while, and, by the way, Johnny was recruited in there. Also I let Johnny off with a warning. For Betty's sake, and I believe he was genuinely sorry for his actions, Willie."

"That sounds like a plan, Johnson, but what about the shadow and night patrols for the Silver Dollar, will you keep them in place now that Johnny has confessed? And I'm in agreement with what you did with Johnny. I truly believe they could have a good life together once he gets an honest job."

"Glad you see it my way. We are going to ease up on the regular car patrols, but the beat cop will continue to pay special attention to the Silver Dollar. As for the shadow, they have been recalled for a special assignment by the top brass."

"Okay, I'll lay low for a few days, Johnson, Joyce and I are going to spend some quiet time together. I am planning to make her Mrs. Jackson soon."

"Nice going, ol' boy, just let me know when and where and I'll be the best man."

"I'm glad Sam Prince is not here; I've never heard of two best men for the same wedding."

"I catch your drift, Willie."

After hanging up the phone, I called out to Joyce and proposed to her with the engagement ring I picked up from a Bay Street store about a week ago. She accepted the ring gladly. After giving me a kiss she left the bedroom.

I thought I was in dreamland when a naked woman woke me up, and was more than pleased when I realized it was not a dream, but my sweet love doll, Joyce. And she was fever-pitched for some sexual satisfaction.

As we made passionate love, it took my mind back to the first time we made out, and now it seemed that time was repeating itself.

"Ooooh! Darling," Joyce moaned as I sank deeper into a pool of sweet sensation. But as my journey came to an end, the calm sea turned into a raging ocean, and I held tightly onto Joyce for fear of going overboard.

Now that calmer seas prevailed I said, "You could wake me up any time for a session like that, doll."

Joyce smiled her satisfaction and we fell into the land of dreams.

Chapter 11

L ast night was a hell of a night; every fiber of my being was worked to a very sensational fulfilment. I guess it was my reward from the excitement Joyce was feeling after I'd asked her to marry me.

It was around 3:00 p.m. when we left the bed and showered together and the warm water took most of the aches from my body. Joyce and I were decked out in all-white attire when we left the house.

I decided to get takeout from the restaurant down at Forster Street and Byrd Road, so Joyce and I climbed into the Charger for the short drive just up the street from our homestead.

As we entered the establishment a slim waitress with a broad smile that signalled "welcome" came over and escorted us to a corner table, then handed us two menus and gave us time to peruse them before asking,

"How may I help you all today?" in a pleasant tone of voice. She reminded me of my waitress Cindy.

"I'll have the steak with peas and rice and potato salad," I replied and passed her the menu. She took it and turned her attention to Joyce, who with a smiling face said, "I'll have the steamed crawfish, peas and rice, and macaroni and cheese."

After accepting the menu from Joyce, she asked, "Anything to drink?"

"Yes, I'll have a Coke," Joyce replied. Then asked, "Anything for you, darling?"

"Ginger ale," I replied, before I glanced around at the small crowd who were stuffing their faces with enjoyable treats.

After giving the waitress a big tip, we collected our food and I drove to the Western Esplanade and parked under a cool tree.

After enjoying our meal, we decided to walk the beach for a while and burn off some of the calories.

The aquamarine water was calm as a light breeze blew inland from across the North Atlantic.

Out in the harbor, a few cruise ships were berthing at the Prince George Dock while two wave runners crisscrossed each other, as a snow white mega-yacht made its way out to the open sea from Nassau Harbor. Joyce and I had gone a good distance from where the Charger was parked.

Time had passed by swiftly and the sun was setting as we made our way back. All but one car was still parked where I had left it, and the couple were enjoying the pleasures of the flesh. The low moans and groans emanating from the vehicle grew louder, followed by some obscenities as we climbed into the Charger. Now that's a good way to get rid of any calories, I told myself.

After closing her car door, Joyce turned her starry eyes on me as her hand reached for my fly. I stopped it and said, "Later, doll." She let out a giggle, and said, "Just trying you, Willie, I am too worn out from last night."

"Ha ha ha, love doll, you are the best," I said and gave her a big passionate kiss. As the entertainment concluded next to us, the happy couple drove off.

The Silver Dollar was in full swing when we arrived. I knew I had told them I was taking time off, but I had to see them in person to give them the news of my plans to wed Joyce.

After a couple of stingers and rum and Cokes, Joyce and I told the staff about our intentions and showed off her engagement ring as we watched their eyes light up. Martha started to cry, Cindy began to sniffle, and Joe had a broad smile on his face.

"Congratulations to both of you," Joe said.

"Congratulations and all the best," Martha and Cindy said together.

"Thanks," I replied and took a stinger while Joyce got a rum and Coke for the road after I paid the tab and left a tip for Joe.

Chapter 12

T he general elections were drawing near and the campaign engines were in full gear. I did not put too much interest in that sort of thing. I knew which party I supported and I knew how to mark my 'X.' While at home, I turned on the TV to catch the evening news.

"Would you like something to snack on while I fix dinner, Willie?" Joyce asked before stepping into the kitchen.

"A corned beef on rye with a tall glass of lemonade will do just fine, doll," I replied as I stretched out to get more comfortable in the settee.

There was not much on the news tonight with the exception of the piece about a dead male and female body being found in a vehicle in the Clifford Park area. It was further stated that an early morning jogger made the gruesome discovery. The police are investigating.

Joyce brought my treat and it tasted good. I changed the channel and began to watch a John Wayne flick. As the movie progressed, my sixth sense began to nag at me and I had no clues as to what might have brought on the nagging.

Three quarters into the movie, Joyce came and sat beside me and the sweet fragrance emanating from her knocked my senses back in order.

"Damn, doll, you smell wonderful," I said, complimenting her.

"Thanks, Willie," she replied, and I saw the light dim in her eyes as her breathing became uneven and warm as we kissed. I quickly got up and went to the bathroom. The water was nice and I washed away whatever discomfort I was feeling, and was surprised when I exited the bathroom and met Joyce in bed with a thin white sheet covering her nude body that revealed all the contours of her shapely figure.

The adventures Joyce puts me through seem to go up a notch every time we enjoyed the pleasures of the flesh. In my book she was made especially for me. But on a more serious note I knew I had to put Jason six feet under before we could live in peace.

That night as I drifted into a sound slumber, Jason Wright invaded my dreams and his pale face showed the hate and contempt he held in his evil heart for me, as he sat down at my table while I was having cocktails at the Silver Dollar, and his bodyguards stood behind him.

"What can I do for you, you piece of horse shit?" I asked sarcastically with my hand under the table.

"I am going to make you pay for fucking my life up, Willie, you son o' bitch!" Jason shouted, getting up from the table as his face turned red.

"Your words don't add up to a hill of beans, hunky. Now get lost before I plant my size 10 up your rear end," I said as one of his goons reached for his piece which was inside his shoulder holster. I brought Betsy from under the table and said, "Make my day, sucker."

I thought I was still dreaming when I heard Joyce's voice calling out to me from a distance. Jason and his men faded from sight as my eyes opened from the shaking she was giving me.

"Wake up, darling, you are talking to Jason in your sleep," Joyce informed me with a worried look on her face.

"Sorry for disturbing you, doll, that sucker is like a vampire out for my blood, but very soon I'm going to take him out permanently with a stake through his evil heart in the form of a .38 slug from Betsy."

Joyce gave me a half smile as she cuddled up to me and drifted back to sleep. Around 6:00 a.m. that nagging sixth sense was back again and woke me from my sleep. It was telling me that I knew the occupants who were found dead on Clifford Park, so to put the matters to rest I went to the front room, picked up the horn, and slowly dialled Sgt. Johnson's home number.

"Hello, Johnson speaking." His voice held a bit of anger.

"Sorry to wake you, ol' boy, but I was curious about the couple found dead in that car on Clifford Park."

"No need for apology, I was up from 4:30 a.m., hardly slept a wink, Willie," Johnson said surprisingly. "Now here it comes."

"Okay, Johnson, lay the cold facts on me."

"That lovely young Betty Wright and her boyfriend were shot in their foreheads from point-blank range with a .22 caliber. Also, we believe they were killed somewhere else and taken to the park."

"Oh my Lord, I wonder why, Johnson?"

"Your guess is as good as mine. Want to give it a shot? No pun intended, Willie."

"I believe they may have been bumped off because someone did not believe their story."

"Make sense, Willie."

"Remember Johnny was picked up and then taken to your headquarters, maybe that event could have spooked his benefactor whom we believe is Prince Brown, and his answers he gave may not have been believable. So they took him out along with his girl because she was with him at the time. So they figure she knew too much so they left no loose ends."

"By damn, I believe you are on to something there, Willie."

"So what are we going to do about it, Johnson?" I asked, then went on to say, "Johnny may have turned some wrong corners, but to take him and his gal out execution style was atrocious."

"I'm getting a hard-on for Prince Brown and will be sending in a couple of officers undercover to the Pussy Cat's Lair in a couple of hours to check the place out before we hit the joint."

"That's a good idea, Johnson. When you get the shit together then I'll make that journey with y'all."

"Okay, Willie, see you later."

Chapter 13

I never liked those big church weddings because they don't last long, so I decided my front room was perfect. So after contacting Judge Rolle, a distant cousin of mine, he gladly consented to do the honors. Mary's catering service was hired, and they came down to get the instructions for the menu. So after preparing a small guest list Joyce and I awaited the caterer.

Kathy and Linda along with their cousin Florance had flown in two days before the wedding and took Joyce to Kathy's residence. They said we should be apart until the day of our wedding.

Finally the waiting was over, and Joyce's arrival took my breath away. Damn she was even lovelier than before.

As a warm Bahamian sun slowly crossed the light blue sky, while Joyce and I were joined as one until death do us part.

"That's for you, Your Honor," I said and slid Judge Rolle an envelope with a grand inside for services rendered.

"It's on the house, Willie," he said, putting the envelope in my inner jacket pocket. "It was my pleasure to unite you two lovebirds."

"Okay, but I insist that you take home two of the Dom Pérignon 1996. And while you're at it carry some of the beluga and lobster tails. We can't let them waste because the setup is costing me a bundle."

"Willie, you are too kind," Judge Rolle replied as he sipped the champagne in his glass.

"Always to friend and families. Okay, now everybody eat, drink, and be merry. The most beautiful bride in the world and I insist."

"Three cheers for the newlyweds," Johnson shouted. "Hip Hip Hip Hooray. Hip Hip Hip Hooray. Hip Hip Hip Horray."

The wedding celebration lasted until a quarter to one a.m. The caterers received their check with a sizeable tip for a job well done.

A pale moon was at the center of the starry sky when our guests said their good nights. Martha, Cindy, and Joe along with their better halves, and Johnson and his lovely wife along with Kathy, Linda, and Florance, made up the guest list.

"Well, love doll, it's over and no Joe Blow is ever coming between us and that's my promise to you till death do us part."

"Thanks, my darling, and you will always be the center of my world and that's my promise to you for as long as I live."

I fixed fried eggs, bacon, and grits along with two tall glasses of freshly squeezed orange juice for me and my love doll.

"Wake up, sleepyhead, breakfast is served," I said after resting the tray on the bureau and liked the surprised look on her face when she opened her eyes.

"Oh! Darling, thank you," Joyce said, getting out of bed and making her way to the bathroom.

After breakfast Joyce looked at me with tears rolling down her cheeks. "Darling," she said, "I feel like I'm living a dream; but thanks to you, I know it's a reality."

"You betcha, doll, and always remember your wishes are my command."

"Only one I have . . ." Joyce paused, and went on to say, "Make a mother out of me, Willie."

"Ha ha ha ha ha!" I roared with laughter and saw the smile vanish from her face.

"I didn't mean for it to be a joke, Willie," she said with a hint of anger in her voice.

"No, doll, I'm not laughing at what you said, I'm laughing at what I thought you might have said."

The warm smile returned to her face and Joyce said, "Please explain what you are thinking about, darling."

"I thought you were about to ask for the moon on a silver platter."

"Oh, you silly man!" Joyce exclaimed. "Come now and let's start the ball rolling so I may have our Lil' Willie."

"Your servant hears and will obey, love doll."

Chapter 14

A day after the wedding my loyal customers got a treat. Free liquor and food was served from 7:00 until at 10:15 p.m. the night.

At half past 11:00 p.m. the place was cleaned and ready for tomorrow's business.

After saying their good nights, Martha, Cindy, and Joe exited the Silver Dollar and Joyce sat in the spot at the bar where she had sat the night of our first encounter. Now she had shares in the establishment as the owner's wife.

"What will it be, Mrs. Willie Jackson?" I asked with a smile. "Your humble servant is ready to do your bidding."

"Rum and Coke, Mr. Willie Jackson," she replied with a smile that illuminated my world.

I got her the rum and Coke and made a stinger for myself, and after passing the drink I said a toast to love and friendship for all eternity.

"Here, here," Joyce replied as our glasses clinked together.

I made a quick check of the door and windows before switching off the lights, but as I exited the joint with Joyce close behind two gunshots rang out from across the street, breaking the stillness of the night.

"Stay inside, Joyce, and take cover," I shouted as I hurried back inside the Silver Dollar.

Joyce raced to the kitchen, almost falling over a chair as I retrieved the pump-action shotgun from under the bar counter, which was kept there for protection in the event of a hold-up.

After arming myself I turned off the outside lights and sneaked through the northern door, and from my vantage point I did not see anything out of the ordinary. I believed that the shooter was long gone by now.

Joyce had remained calm through the whole ordeal. I guess being around Jason for so long, she might have experienced lots of different action to which she had to self-adjust to.

Back home Joyce and I were tempted to continue to work on that assignment she had given me, but the shooter was on my damn mind and it spoiled things for me in the sex department for the time being.

Johnson answered the telephone on the first ring.

"Hello."

"I have some disturbing news for you, old friend."

"Let me have it, Willie."

"Someone took a couple of shots at me when Joyce and I were leaving our business place. By the way, are we still on the radar?"

"Yes and no. The upcoming election which is due soon has our manpower stretched thin. So we are doing the best we can with a car passing by at intervals in that area."

"Okay I could buy that, so what about that shooter?"

"Making an official complaint, Willie?"

"That won't be necessary, chalk it up as police information. Maybe it's Jason having his goons fuck with my head while he masturbates in his prison cell. The bullets were a bit wild. They went over my head."

"Get some sleep and we will link up in the morning, Willie."

"Okay we have a date, Sergeant."

My velvety smooth and beautiful wife was a true treasure. Her warm lips and powder-sugar tongue heightened my desires for what came next. To hell with the aggravation going through my mind. The cure was next to me in the bed. Joyce fell asleep and I lay awake letting my mind reminisce on the events that took place after we became lovers. The trials and tribulations that followed were from the high-speed chase after Jason's goons abducted Joyce from my home, which led to gun battles at his mansion, and finally Sgt. Johnson put Jason before the court where he was sent to the government institute for the insane. Now he was finishing that stretch in Her Majesty's Prison. And the son o' bitch was making my life a living hell from his cell.

The telephone dismissed the trend of thoughts from my mind as it begged for attention.

"Hello, Mr. Jackson," the female voice greeted me when I placed the receiver to my ears.

I could not put a name or face to the voice, but it sounded familiar.

"How may I help you, Miss?" My words were sincere.

"My name is Elizabeth Culmer," she said, then paused to see if I had any recollection of her. After sensing that I was drawing a blank, she went on to say, "It was me who forced you to go to the Pussy Cat's Lair."

I began to see red as that bad memory returned to my mind in a flash. She sensed something was wrong, then quickly interjected, "I can't say how sorry I am, Mr. Jackson, but I was duped into taking you captive. Prince Brown said he had a few questions that needed some answers. He swore to me violence was out of the question, and it was going to be a peaceful chat. Cross my heart hope to die."

"What about the bounty you collected for my head?"

"Like I said, sir, I was told that it was a question-and-answer situation. Sometime later that night I found out

I was lied to. You must believe me. If I had known his ulterior motive, I wouldn't have taken the job."

Her voice went soft and my sixth sense did not give a warning, so I believed what she had told me was the truth.

"Let's say I believe you, what is it you want now?"

"Prince Brown is covering his tracks and has begun to eliminate anyone who could connect him to you, Mr. Jackson."

"I put one and one together when Johnny and his gal were terminated, I knew they would be coming for me."

"Mr Jackson, I have some information in my possession that I came across some time ago. Which may be of some help to you. Meet me on the corner of Thatch Palm Ave. and Bamboo Boulevard near the church and the convenience store. By the way are you familiar with that location?"

"Yes."

"Okay, I'll be inside a white car, license number 6759."

"Okay, Liz, I'm on my way."

Chapter 15

W hen I hung up from Elizabeth Culmer, I dialled Sgt. Johnson's number and I brought him up to date on what Elizabeth had told me.

My love doll was asleep when I left, so I took Betsy along with a few extra rounds in case I ran into the unexpected.

After travelling south on East Street I made a left onto Sapodilla Boulevard and took the second right into Thatch Palm Avenue, then eased my way towards my destination.

The atmosphere was quiet at 2:00 a.m. until a dog began to howl as an ambulance raced eastwardly along Bamboo Boulevard, its siren signalling there was an emergency service needed to be rendered to some poor soul.

On reaching Elizabeth's parked car, I saw when a bald-headed black man with a limp ran from it with a large white envelope and climbed inside a dark vehicle, which drove off as the Charger drew near.

Blam! Blam!

Two gunshots were fired from the fleeing car in my direction. I then brought the Charger to a complete halt and got out in quick time to bust off a cap from Betsy but to no avail. The fleeing car made a sharp right turn onto Bamboo Boulevard, its tire screeching from the sudden turn on the asphalt as they made their getaway. Elizabeth was bleeding from her nose in a semi-conscious state when I entered her vehicle.

"Who did this to you, Elizabeth?" I asked with compassion for someone who was once the enemy. "Was it Prince Brown?"

"It was, and he got the package."

"What was in it?"

"It was instructions from Jason to take out you, your wife, and Sgt. Johnson. Along with some of his friends who had turned their backs on him. Most importantly, it was about the release of . . . ." Elizabeth paused, and said, "Lord it hurts."

I did not see the gunshot wound to her chest because she was hiding it with her hand. Minutes later Johnson and two other cops pulled up on the scene as I was about to exit Elizabeth's vehicle.

"Come out with your hands up," a voice barked. "And no funny stuff or I'll blow your ass to kingdom come."

"He's the one who tipped me off, Cartwright. He is on our side. Now put away your weapon," Johnson ordered. Cartwright did as ordered so Johnson went on to say, "Call the undertaker and get this deceased to the morgue ASAP so the pathologist can do his thing. Also, contact Cpl. Pinder and have him impound this vehicle for the lab boys to go over, and Cartwright, tell Pinder to make haste."

While Cartwright took care of business, Johnson and I went to my vehicle and sat a while.

"Give me your gut feeling on this matter, Willie. Too many people dropping down like dead flies."

"My gut is telling me that it ain't long now for the bubble burst and the stink will hit the fan," I replied, looking at the starry sky, and I could have sworn I heard Elizabeth say she's safe now when I saw a twinkling star, which seemed to shine more brightly in the cluster of the heavenly bodies as if to say, "See me here. I'm where I belong."

Johnson, who was looking up at the sky, said, "The sky is full of stars tonight," before turning his attention to me, saying, "First it was Johnny and Betty, now it's Elizabeth Culmer, and we know they all had one link in common, Prince Brown."

"Hell, he just got away by the skin of his teeth. My car has one front headlight. The right front light because the other was shot out by someone in the getaway car," I said.

"By the way, Liz told me that Jason is planning to take you, me, and Joyce out, and some of his old political buddies for turning their backs on him."

"I hear you talking, Willie, but those punks don't frighten me one bit. So I will suggest we wait until after the election and bring down Prince Brown and all other suckers who will follow him. Because when they fuck with the Serge, they have bought themselves a one-way ticket to hell."

"Now you are speaking my language, good buddy . . . but I'm sorry Sam Prince is not here. Him and I did teach Jason a thing or two the first time we tangoed."

"Yeah, shit Willie, you two boys helped me send that sucker away to the funny farm. And cleaned up that stockpile of guns and ammunition he had stored in his mansion."

Joyce was still asleep when I returned at a quarter to four—or at least I thought she was; that's why I was taken by surprise when I heard . . .

"Hello, darling, is everything alright? I got up earlier and found you gone."

"Go back to sleep, doll, and I will fill you in later."

"Whatever you say, love of my life, once I know you are safe then I'm okay."

Chapter 16

T he following day the government had changed. The People's Justice Movement had wrestled the reins of power from the Progressive People's Party. It was the first time in twenty years that the Progressive People's Party tasted defeat, and it was joy and celebration for the party and its supporters that sat in opposition for so many years.

It was 9:30 p.m. when Joyce had showered and slipped into a sexy see-through negligee, then joined me in the love seat and I filled her in on the events that had happened the night before, when Elizabeth was killed.

"So what does all this add up to, Willie?" Joyce asked. "And what could have been in that envelope that caused a life to be taken?"

"Your guess is as good as mine, Joyce, who could figure out Jason's sick mind?" I replied, withholding what Elizabeth had told me about the death threats and Jason's impending release from prison.

"Willie, I'm scared, I have a feeling that somehow Jason is going to get his revenge on us. And I believe he will do horrible things to us before we die."

"There may be some truth in your words, but don't be afraid, darling, this time I'll send him to his grave whenever he moves toward us, and that's a promise to bank on. Because there is a bullet in Betsy that's got Jason written all over it."

Joyce threw her arms around me and said, "I knew when I first laid eyes on you, you were the right man for me, Willie."

Joyce's words sent warm shivers racing up and down my spine. But as much as I hate to mention it, I had to take my hat off to that son o' bitch, Jason Wright, because he was the cause of Joyce and I getting together in the first place.

"You are one in a million, love doll, every time I am feeling a bit down you find the right words to cheer me up."

"Glad to be of help, darling."

I took my lovely wife in my arms and gave her a passionate kiss. But when I tried to pull away she held me back, saying, "I felt some tension as you held me, darling, and it frightened me."

"The tension can't be helped, doll. That beating Prince Brown laid on me was the beginning and not the ending of some diabolical hatred he and Jason have in their hearts for me. Now they have written checks none of the suckers could cash. Because when they entered my space without invitation signed and sealed by me the rules were changed, and they had sign their own death warrant."

Joyce loosened her hold and the sadness left her face; she must have found solace in my words and she said, "Kick some ass, Willie, and make Jason regret ever hearing your name."

I felt new energy flow through every fiber of my being. After my love doll's charge had rejuvenated me, I told her, "It's a promise. Even if I have to take out all of the goons one by one to get to him, I will get the job done in spades."

Joyce left the love seat and I followed her into the bedroom. The clock on the wall showed a quarter to 1:00 a.m. as we sailed through an ocean of bliss.

Sleep came easy for me as I rolled off my love doll, and, as always, she had given me a sexual workout that satisfied my body and mind.

Chapter 17

The loud knocking on my front door got me out of bed in a hurry. And after putting on my bathrobe, I took the revolver from the bureau drawer and put it in the robe's right pocket.

"Who is it?" I called out.

"It's me, Willie," Sgt. Johnson replied.

I opened the door and Johnson entered the house with a facial expression I was not accustomed to. He looked dejected, so I braced myself for what was to follow.

After taking a seat in the armchair he said, "Fix me a rum and Coke, Willie, and go easy on the soda. This is one of those days I feel useless and worn out."

"What brings that on, ol' buddy? Lay it on me hard, I'm a big boy and could take the punishment," I said while mixing the drinks.

Johnson put the glass to his mouth and drank a good bit of the mixture. Before looking me in the eyes and saying, "My undercover men informed me that the Pussy Cat's Lair doesn't exist."

I choked on my drink, and after regaining my composure I said, "Run that by me again, Johnson."

"They said when they arrived at the location, a pastor was holding church service."

"You are pulling my legs, Johnson. Let's go see if this is the same place. Your boys must have visited the wrong address," I said as I went into the bedroom and put on some street clothing before giving Joyce a kiss.

A warm sun was making its way to the center of the light blue sky.

When Johnson introduced me to Detective Constable Roy Moss, a slim-built, dark-complexioned chap who looked to be in his mid-20's. Later I found out that Moss was one of the officers who had brought Johnson the information about the Pussy Cat Lair transformation.

After the introduction, I climbed into the backseat and got a quick flashback of those good old days I had spent working in the Mobile Division.

The sun was now crossing the sky as we made our way to South Beach along the route Elizabeth and I had taken when I made my first journey to the Pussy Cat's Lair.

I almost let rip a few cuss words after we entered the now "Church of the Living Savior."

The pool table, the bar, even the kitchen was a thing of the past. Prince Brown's office was now the official office of Rev. Samuel B. Roker.

"My brothers, may I be of service?" a short fat man wearing thick glasses asked. "My name is Rev. Roker. Samuel B. Roker, and whom may I have the pleasure of welcoming to the Lord's House?"

Johnson showed his warrant card and I reached my hand to Rev. Roker for a shake. He took it and I said, "Willie Jackson, pleased to meet you, Rev. Roker."

"The pleasure is all mine, my brothers, do step inside my office, I'm always pleased to welcome one and all into the house of the Lord, especially our law enforcement officers."

Cold bumps came over my flesh when I walked into what used to be Brown's office. Rev. Roker must have sensed my discomfort and said, "God is good. Nothing here will do you harm, Mr. Jackson."

"Thank you, Rev. My mind had wandered off a bit," I said and watched Rev. smile before saying, "Do have a seat, gentlemen." The desk Rev. Rocker was sitting behind was new. There was no evidence that Brown ever had use of the place.

"Now, please, tell me how I may be of service, gentlemen," Rev. Roker asked with a saintly smile on his face.

I listened intently as Sgt. Johnson put questions to him about the previous owner and saw that Rev. Roker was a bit uneasy when he told the story of a man with a limp who came to his small wooden church on Augusta Street and presented him the deeds for the building and a manager's check for twenty thousand dollars. As a donation to help with the restructuring of the building. Johnson and I knew he was referring to Prince Brown. Rev. Roker further stated his benefactor said that the Lord had come to him in a dream, and, the rest, is history.

Johnson then tried to find out if the man with the limp left any calling card or ever came to any of his services, and Rev. Roker answered "no" to both questions. Johnson then pressed on, asking Rev. Rocker if he didn't see anything suspiciously wrong by the sudden gift he had received from a total stranger. And he responded to Johnson by letting him know the Lord works in mysterious ways. With that saying we bid Rev. good-bye.

As the car pulled onto the main road, I said, "Something stinks all the way to heaven around there, Johnson, and it's not the dead fish at Potters Cay Dock.

"I smell it too, Willie, so let's use a larger hook, because I aim to catch a big, live sucker fish goes by the name of Prince Brown," Johnson said assuringly.

"Yes and use a short line. I'm down with you all the way, my brother, and I'm going to bait the hook with a stink-smelling cigar that rat fish Prince Brown can't refuse.

Now let's go to the Silver Dollar. I need a strong drink to settle my nerves."

"A stiff drink about now sounds good, Willie."

Unbeknown to Johnson and I, back at the church, the toilet flushed in the male bathroom and Prince Brown and two of his boys exited the restroom and went into Rev. Roker's office.

"They came as you expected, Mr. Brown. I believe your ploy threw them in a tailspin," Rev. Roker said happily.

"You may be right, but now that you have accomplished that goal for me, you have made yourself expendable."

Rev. Roker didn't know what struck him from behind, but he fell to the floor with a cracked skull from the piece of iron pipe Wallace bashed him with.

A few people were in the Silver Dollar when we arrived. Johnson had his rum and Coke and I tried to relax with a double stinger. Moss drank a Coke. He told us he'd sworn off the booze a year ago.

As James Brown's voice filled the Silver Dollar's atmosphere, my neighbor entered and took a seat at the bar. She was much prettier in daylight. After excusing myself from the table, I went behind the bar.

"Hello Rita, I see you finally made it."

"Yes, Willie. I'm here to cash in my rain check," she said with a smile that revealed a dimple in both jaws.

"You heard the lady, Joe, give her what she wants and put it on my tab."

"Okay, boss!" Joe exclaimed excitedly.

Before returning to my chair, I said, "I'm sitting with friends, care to join us?"

"Don't mind if I do, bartender, I'll have a screwdriver, please," Rita said before making her way to where Johnson and Moss was sitting.

"One screwdriver coming up," Joe said.

After the introduction we were one big family sharing conversations and party jokes, as someone punched the jukebox and the O Jay's "Backstabbers" replaced James Brown's "Please Don't Go."

The four of us had a swell time, and as we were about to get up from the table, Rita smiled and asked, "How is Mrs. Jackson?"

"She's fine, Rita, thanks for inquiring, maybe one day you two should have lunch, I believe you two may have much in common."

"Thanks, I'll appreciate meeting her, Willie," Rita said. Her voice was seductive and if it wasn't for the drinks, I'd think she was flirting with me. We finished our party and said our good-byes.

Joyce had made spaghetti and meatballs, one of my favorite dishes. But my stomach couldn't handle another morsel.

"Would you care for something to eat now, darling."

"I'm afraid Martha's fish-and-chips have me overstuffed."

"Okay, darling, I'll put it up for later."

"Sounds good, love doll. I'm going to hit the shower. Care to join me?"

"Now you're talking my language, Willie," Joyce cooed.

Chapter 18

At a quarter to 1:00 a.m. Joyce woke me up with a frightening look on her face, saying, "Darling, you were tossing violently in your sleep and mumbling words I couldn't understand for the exception of Jason's name."

"I was having a bad dream, doll."

"What was the dream about, Willie?"

"Two of Jason's men held me while that lowlife burned me with his half-smoked cigarette."

"I'm happy it was only a dream, now let me ease that pressure on your mind."

"I'm beginning to feel better already, love doll."

Joyce was right as usual: her warm body and hot tongue put all my ills in the trash bin of forgotten time.

I climbed out of bed half past 6:00 a.m. because of the loud knocking on the front door.

After calling out and not receiving any answer, ever so slowly I opened the door with my left hand while I held the .38 revolver in the right. I was shocked by the sight that greeted me, which sent shivers through my entire body, causing me to almost regurgitate last night's meal.

The decapitated dog's head that was left on my porch was not a sight for sore eyes. I quickly got some disinfectant liquid, a pair of gloves, and placed the head inside a garbage bag before calling Johnson and bringing him up to date on the happening."

"Say what, Willie, someone left a dog's head on your porch?"

"That's correct, Johnson."

"Okay I'll be on my way soon as I deal with matters at hand, Willie."

"Take your time, Johnson, I know how it is when you scrap one ol' man. You must make good use of it."

"Go to hell, Willie, see you when I see you ha ha ha ha."

"Yeah, next half hour suits me fine."

Johnson laughed again before turning his attention to Mrs. Johnson, who began to smile as she readied herself for her husband's penetration.

Half an hour later, Johnson was on my porch looking in the garbage bag.

"Have you seen any animal around your neighborhood lately that might fit this head, Willie?"

"I don't think so, Johnson."

"I'll take the head so the boys can take a photo of it, and while I'm at it check to see if anyone had reported a missing dog matching this poor creature's description and hope it gives us a lead on who could have done this hideous deed. Even though all signs may be pointing to Prince Brown's doorstep.

"Willie, I'm going to have a car patrol around here and your business place more often until this matter is settled one way or the other, dig?"

"I dig, Sergeant, by the way, I'm sending Joyce to her sister in Miami out of harm's way."

"You must have read my mind, Willie, I was just about to suggest the same thing. See you at the Silver Dollar around 2:00 p.m."

I returned to the bedroom after Johnson left and met Joyce taking a sip of red wine from the half-filled glass and said, "Morning, doll." And, after getting no response I quickly asked, "Darling, are you alright?"

"Oh! What? Willie, I'm sorry I was reminiscing about the past and had the urge for some crushed grapes."

"Yes I saw the blank expression on your face, now tell me what's bugging you, doll?"

"I'm fine, darling. How about something to eat, Willie? I'm starved."

"Not now, doll, but there is something I want to run by you."

"Go ahead, darling, you have my undivided attention."

The glass was now empty and I saw a look of excitement in her eyes, so I did not expect the reply I received when I told her, "Love doll, I'm sending you to Florida to be with Kathy until this mess is taken care of."

"Not on your sweet life, Willie Jackson. A wife's place is with her husband in times of trouble. End of discussion."

I recovered quickly and tried a different approach as I took the glass from her and rested it on the bureau.

"Come now, love doll, you know I don't want anything bad happening to you."

"Ha ha ha," Joyce laughed, then went on to say, "okay, darling, you win. I'll make the contact with Kathy and leave incognito. But for how long?"

"There's no time limit on this melting pot. But I figure a week and a half at most."

"Okay, Willie, but see if you can conclude within a week."

The deal with my doll was signed and sealed; now it was time for me to deliver. But I got my wish. She was leaving and I was happy. Now Jason and his underlords would be getting a full dose of pure TNT exploding up their asses.

Chapter 19

I went down to the Silver Dollar to meet Sgt. Johnson as planned, but he did not show so I took the opportunity to let the staff know that from today Martha would be running the establishment day to day. I also let them know that Joyce went to visit her sister in Florida, and only in case of emergencies was I to be reached. After downing two stingers, I waved my good-byes.

Back home I dialled Sgt. Johnson's office number and he picked up on the first ring.

"You missed our date today, buddy. What caused the no-show?"

"A thousand pardons, Willie, but something smoking was placed on my desk, and it may have my attention for a day or two."

"What's going on, pal?"

"Rev. Roker's dead body was found in his house on Augusta Street after one Carla Roach, a next-door neighbor, reported that there was a stink odor emanating from his blue and white house. And get this, he was not a Rev. but a con man by the name of Sammy Strachan. 'Roker' was an alias."

"Any leads? By the way, Joyce has left for Florida. So the coast is clear for warfare."

"Someone reported seeing a blue car with two black male occupants drive away from Strachan's residence two nights ago, which would be shortly after our visit with him the other day, and I'm glad Joyce is out of harm's way and I am heating up the war drum as we speak."

"My money is on Prince Brown. Have you and your men made a return trip to the church to see if any evidence was left laying around?"

"Yes and no."

"Stop tickling my foot, Serge."

"The damn building no longer exists, Willie. Someone put fire to it and only a shell of its former structure is still standing."

"Well I'll be the son of a pole cat. Now those cockroaches are in hiding."

"I get your drift, Willie. So we have to use a super insecticide to flush the sons o' bitches out of their crawlspace."

"You betcha. So that we can squash them under our heels."

Jason Wright, the little white pretty boy with lots of money, was sending his orders from behind the cold steel bars of his prison cell. While being pampered with good food and the best wines money could buy from those guards who could be bought.

Forgiveness was not in his vocabulary. His evil mind had come to one conclusion. Get revenge on the man who'd entered his world, killed off his men, and won the heart of his beloved Joyce Collie; now the prison bars that caged him would not be a deterrent from his wishes coming through.

A smile toyed at my lips when thoughts of Jason Wright entered my head. Because I always knew our destiny would put us on a collision course to hell. The Rolls Royce or the Dodge Charger. Who will come out alive after the big crash? My bet was on me one hundred to one percent. I beat him once and I'll beat him again. Only this time it will be for all the marble.

It must have been around 3:40 a.m. when the telephone rang. Half asleep, I picked it up.

"Yes."

"Hey, good buddy, remember me?"

"At this ungodly hour with a head full of sleep, how can I make out a voice that I'm not too familiar with?"

"My apologies, Mr. Jackson, but one good turn deserves another."

"Skip the bullshit and go fuck yourself."

Click. The phone went dead. I closed my eyes and tried to get back to the dream I was having about Joyce and I making out on a white sandy beach. If I ever find the caller I'll strangle . . . the rest of my thoughts were cut off when the phone rang again.

"No bullshit, Mr. Jackson. Jason Wright is out of prison and he's hunting for you with blood in his eyes."

The caller now had my full attention after Jason's name was mentioned.

"Come on, friend, give me your name and make my day." The hostility was out of my voice and I was ready for what he was going to throw at me.

"Okay, you deserve to know. I'm the guy you returned the 500 bucks to after you realized that I had no intentions of harming Joyce."

"No shit, Charles Lloyd, is that you? Man I figured you had skipped town for good."

"I was laying low in Inagua for a while, but after you sent Jason to the slammer I returned back to New Providence and kept a low profile. Doing a little of this and that to survive. Maybe I may be of service to you. I'm low on cash and my bookie is on my ass like a fly on shit. Plus I have a hot broad to bang who likes nose candy."

"If you are on the up and up, like I believe you are, there is a grand in for you, Charles."

"You are talking my language, Mr. Jackson. The bookie gets half and the fine little gal I'll spend the other half on, dig?"

"Okay, Charles, meet me here tonight at 8:00 p.m.

"I'll be there, Mr. Jackson."

"It's Willie to friends."

"Okay, Willie, see you soon with a head full of goodies to lay on you."

"I'm all ears, Charles, see you when you get here."

Was it luck or was it one of Jason's ploys to get my strength and weakness. After I hung up from Charles I dialled Johnson's home number and I hoped he was not still tied down with Strachan's case. Because I wanted him to hear what Charles had to say.

"I'm tired of disturbing your sleep, Serge, but this is a piece of hot coal you don't want to throw water on yet."

"Give me a second, Willie. I need to take a piss." That second ran into a few minutes, then Johnson came back on the line. "Okay, Willie, bring me up to date on this burning issue."

After telling Johnson about Jason's surprise release from prison and the deal I made with Charles Lloyd, he said he would get to me before Charles arrived.

Chapter 20

Sergeant Johnson arrived at a quarter to 8:00 p.m. and we waited for Charles Lloyd together.

"What in the hell is going on, Willie? How could Jason Wright's time get cut so short? At the outset he was given 15 years. He was in the mental hospital for 3 ½ years and has only served the 2 years in prison. Totalling 5 ½ years."

"Maybe we will get that answer when Charles arrives."

"I hope so," Johnson exclaimed as he made himself a rum and Coke. "Care to join me, Willie?" Before I could answer the telephone rang.

"Willie here, how may I help you?" I heard myself say into the mouthpiece.

"Lose the dickhead or the deal is off," Charles told me in an undertone.

"Who are you speaking about, Charles?" I played the fool.

"The one who parked his vehicle around the corner and walked to your house. Man I have a rap sheet about a mile long and some friends in prison waiting to beat my ass for scamming them out of lots of dough. Dig? And before they are let loose in the free world, I want to be able to make things right with them."

"Come on in from the cold, Charles, he's a very good friend; and like me, he also needs to know what you have to offer first hand."

"Only if you can guarantee I will be untouchable from the man . . ." Charles paused, before saying, "Now do you dig where I am coming from, my brother? That kind of heat I don't need in my life right now, Mr. Jackson."

"Hold the line, Charley," I said, then relayed the terms to Johnson and he agreed with them. So I told Charles, "You may come in, the flames have gone out. You have become untouchable for the rest of the night."

With a little bit of gray hair on his head, Charles' facial appearance and body structure had not changed. He still looked like the man standing by the lamppost who I'd brought back to my house with my revolver pressing in his back some years ago. After being sent on an assignment by Jason Wright to harm Joyce.

Charles had told me a lie the first time we met: that he was not working for Jason. But Joyce told me he was really one of Jason's enforcers who was used from time to time to deal with someone who stepped out of line, and see that they marched to the beat of Jason's drum.

"Okay, my brothers, you may ask me any question, and if I have the correct answers, I'll lay it on you; but Willie my man, first things first."

"What's that, Charles?" I played the fool again.

"The bread, man, you know the green cabbage you promised me, dig?"

I placed the half ground in his outstretched hand, then said, "The other half will depend on how believable your story is. Now make us proud."

Johnson and I listened intently as Charles told us that Jason pulled in some IOU's from some of his party's bigwigs to get the early release. Prince Brown was responsible for Sammy Strachan, Elizabeth Culmer, and the two dead bodies found on Clifford Park. Charles reached in his waistband and produced a .22 revolver, which he held with a hankie and handed to Johnson, and told him it was the weapon used in the killings. He further stated that he dug it up from Jason's backyard from where Prince Brown had buried it.

"There is a price on Serge's head because of his involvement in Jason's arrest; to my knowledge no one has tried to collect the bounty as yet because crooks have the utmost fear for you. But most of all he wants to make love to Joyce in front of you, Willie, before he has her brutally raped while you watch. Now in your case, Willie, he wants to cut off your balls and stuff them down your throat.

"Also, in a day or two Prince Brown is going to burn down the Silver Dollar and a few of Jason's goons are coming around to bring you and Joyce to him."

"How do you know all this, Charles?" Johnson asked before taking a long drink from the half-filled glass.

"I'm the fly on the wall. I know all the ins and outs of Jason's organization, Sergeant, dig?"

"Where are Jason and Prince Brown located?" Johnson probed further after digesting what Charles had fed him. It tasted like shit but he didn't spit it out.

"Jason has moved back into his mansion, and Prince Brown along with four other men are living on St. Alban's Drive in the Golden Palace. They occupy rooms 16, 17, and 18. Prince Brown is in 17."

"How many men does Jason have at his mansion?" I asked Charles who had lit a cigarette and was blowing O's at the ceiling.

"About six, two were taken out of circulation sometime back. I think they were chasing you and got pulled over by the cops on East Street South."

"How did you know that?" I asked, and as Charles was about to answer, I said, "Forget it."

"By the way, Willie, I was at the Pussy Cat's Lair when Elizabeth brought you there. Do you remember the lovely lady with the big afro? Well I was the guy who got up and went to the jukebox. I didn't want you to recognize me."

I let my mind wander back to the Lair and saw the lady with the afro. Charles was right, her partner did get up and go to play the records.

"He's correct, Johnson, there was a lady with a 'fro and a guy did get up when I entered the Pussy Cat's Lair before I could have made eye contact."

"Anything else I can do for you two gentlemen? If not, I have a hot mama under the sheets waiting for me, get my drift, gentlemen?"

I wanted to laugh, but my destiny was now full circle. I didn't doubt anything Charles had told us so I pulled out the last five bills and passed it to him, saying, "Thanks, Charles, and be careful not to become a casualty of war."

"Right on, brother. Thanks for the dough and advice," Charles said before exiting through the back door and fading into the darkness.

Chapter 21

Johnson and I sat down with rum and Coke in tall glasses while mulling over what Charles Lloyd had laid at our feet. It was a believable tale which needed to be dealt with in short order.

"Shit!" Johnson said, and then drank from his glass. "That Jason Wright must be taken out. He is one piece of trash the human race could do without. In all my days as a policeman, I never thought I would hear myself say that, Willie. But Jason is that kind of lowlife who brings your dark side into the light for scrutiny."

"I get your drift, Johnson, but in actuality it's them or us, the bad versus the good, and serious action needs to be taken as of yesterday to smash Jason and his goons like the vermin they are."

"Today is Friday, by Monday I want this mess cleared away. I'm going to the Market Street Station to have an officer patrol the area during the daytime, and one of my cars will pay special attention to the area after closing time. Down at the Silver Dollar, I have a strong feeling Prince Brown and his boys are going to make their move by weekend."

"Sounds realistic, Johnson, meanwhile I'll start closing the establishment early during the night; by the way, I think you better call off the uniform and stick with the car patrols."

"Why, Willie?" Johnson asked as he scratched an imaginary itch on his forehead.

"Don't want Prince Brown to get spooky and try to burn the Silver Dollar down with people inside. So it would be better to stake out the area with plainclothes officers. That way we will have the upper hand on them."

"By damn, Willie, I read you loud and clear. Shit! I need to retire."

"Why?"

"Every time I raise a good hard-on I don't get a chance to use it anymore. Too many demands this job is putting on me, the stress factor I believe is taking its toll on me. Sometimes I can't even piss straight."

"Sorry if my situation added to your problem, ol' boy."

"Not from you, Willie, your situation don't count, but I must confess all is not lost in the sex department, Mrs. Johnson gets the old boy to stand to attention then he gladly marches in her parade."

"Ha ha ha, Johnson, you are a one-man riot squad. Thanks, buddy, I needed that bit of humor."

Johnson left after finishing one more rum and Coke. He told me he was going home for supper, a shower, and shave. I did the same thing. My leftover spaghetti and meatballs came in handy. It may have been a day or so old, but the damn thing tasted like it had just been cooked. It must be the love Joyce had put into the preparation. Bless her kind heart.

The shower was refreshing as the water sprayed down from the golden showerhead. It was midnight when I went to bed, but sleep was hard to come by because my mind was so mixed up I could not think straight. But the comforting thoughts of knowing that Joyce was safe somehow sent me off into the land of dreams where I found myself face to face with Jason in a coliseum; he was pretending to be Caesar and I was naked as a jay bird, standing chained between two wooden posts.

"You have been found guilty for stealing Caesar's woman and your punishment is castration," Prince Brown read from a parchment; he looked like a son o' bitch in a centurion uniform. He then turned his eye on Jason, who gave the thumbs down. Then with a hellish grin on his ugly mug, Prince went on to say, "Executioner, grab those balls and slice them suckers off!"

"Nooo!" I heard myself cry out as the sun rays reflected off the razor-sharpened knife. But, by some miracle, Joyce led a charge of female warriors into the coliseum, but as she was about to set me free the telephone cried out for attention. And I was more than happy when Joyce said, "Hello darling, I miss you and want to come home."

"I miss you too, but the timing is off. How are Kathy and Linda doing?"

"They are much better than me. I am a basket case with nerves that are on edge, because I need to be in your arms."

"Please bear with the separation for a few more days, Johnson and I will soon have this matter concluded hopefully by weekend."

"Okay, darling, I'll try my best. Bye for now. I love you and I'll see you in my dreams until we are together again."

"Bye, love, you too and I'll do likewise." After Joyce hung up my mind reflected on the dream I'd had, and wondered if we would have made it to safety.

Morning was at hand and I was ready for the unexpected. I went to the Silver Dollar and found business was as usual. A good crowd was on hand having cocktails, and as they conversed the jukebox played one of the late great songs by Roy Hamilton, "You Can Have Her." Which was followed by the Platters' "Smoke Gets in Your Eyes."

I left when Jackie Wilson's "Lonely Teardrops" came on. Damn! Someone had the golden-oldies blues.

I climbed behind the wheel of the Charger and drove to South Beach. I wanted to take a look at the rubble of the Pussy Cat's Lair.

Shit! The damn building was unrecognizable, it was as Johnson had stated, "Just a shell of its former structure."

A cool breeze blowing inland from across South Beach rustled through the trees as I climbed back inside the Charger. The area started to give me the creeps so I beat a hasty retreat.

There were a few cars on the street as I made a right on South Beach Blvd. and got a flashback of the time Elizabeth brought me at gunpoint to Prince Brown. Now I was itching to give him the beating of his life, in diamonds, clubs, and spades, or better yet, let his ass sleep with the fishes.

I could see something was dead wrong when I reached my front door. The small piece of tape I had put down low on the door frame was disturbed. I turned the door knob ever so slowly, and pushed it gently as I stood on the northern corner of the porch with my gun in hand.

Boom! The shotgun blast sent pellets in the air. I then rushed inside and shot the sucker who was sitting at my dining table with the death-maker in his hand. He was someone I had seen when I was taken to the Pussycat's Lair. A smile of satisfaction toyed at my lips knowing I had sent the son o' bitch on a one-way trip straight to hell.

Chapter 22

A neighbor who'd heard the gunshots called the police emergency number and made a report. But before the vehicles which were dispatched to the scene arrived, Johnson's squad car came to a screeching halt in front of my house and exited the vehicle.

"Hey, Willie, are you alright in there?" Johnson called out as his partner hurried to the rear of the building. "Someone reported hearing gunshots coming from your apartment."

"Yes, I'm okay, but I have a present for you," I replied as I opened the front door.

"Nice shot, I see you didn't lose your touch, Willie. You put the bullet dead center of John Matthew's forehead," Johnson said in an adoring tone of voice.

"You knew that lowlife, Serge?" I asked, pointing at the corpse.

"Only by his rap sheet. He had one a mile long. Word on the street was that he was a gun for hire."

"So why wasn't he put away?"

"The sucker was always a step ahead of us; when time for the trials, the witness would disappear or complaints were withdrawn before we could process them.

"But we got his ass on a grievous-harm rap when he almost chopped off his cousin's hand in a dice game. He had claimed his cousin was shooting loaded dice. He got seven years in jail and was later freed after five for good behavior."

"Well I have no regrets for this sucker; he wanted to take me out of circulation permanently."

"I know what you mean, Willie. I have no sympathy for him either."

Detective Constable Moss joined us inside after satisfying himself that all was clear on the outside. Moss had smiled when he saw John sitting in my chair with his head tilted backwards, and he came over and shook my hand for putting a menace out of circulation, causing the underworld to lose a commodity. But lots of innocent people's lives who were caught in the cross fires would be spared now that John Matthew's life had been taken by my bullet. And I was happy to be of help to society.

Two patrol cars pulled up simultaneously with lights flashing and sirens wailing. By that time a small crowd had gathered to see what the excitement was all about. In the meantime, a sergeant from the Uniform Branch entered the house and engaged in a conversation with Johnson.

After their chat, Johnson brought him over and introduced him to me. His name was Rosten Rolle, and they both agreed that it was self-defense. I was placed in Johnson's custody and taken to the Criminal Investigation Department.

The assistant commissioner in charge of the department wanted to pin a medal on me after he was brought up to date by Johnson.

ACP McKenzie, a tall man in his late 50's. Ruled the matter self-defense and returned my revolver to me because I had a special permit to carry a concealed weapon and my gun license was up to date. I got the green light and waved my good-byes.

Down at the Colony Palace, Prince Brown was working up a storm between the sheets with a young woman, and grunting like a pig as he raced to a noisy climax.

"Damn that cunt of yours was the best I fucked in a long while. How would you like to be one of my special lady's?"

"Say the words, big daddy, and the pussy is yours for as long as you want me around."

"What did you say your name was, sweet mama?"

"Carla Sweeting."

"Okay Carla, from now on you belong to me," Prince concluded. But just as she began to give him a blowjob a knock sounded on the door.

"Don't disturb me now!" Prince shouted as Carla's head bobbed up and down on his shaft.

"Sorry, boss, but this is very important," the voice said on the outside.

"It better be, Sidney, or I'll have your head for this intrusion; you know while my lovemaking session is going on my room is off-limits to everyone with the exception of Jason Wright."

Sidney gingerly entered the room and was amazed to see the woman swallow Prince's long shaft down her throat.

"Well?" Prince inquired. But before Sidney could speak, he erupted and withdrew from Carla's mouth, and sprayed his semen over her body while uttering obscenities. Nothing gave him more pleasure than to spray his sperm on a female's body as he talked dirty to her.

Carla's light-brown skin and shapely body turned Sidney on as she climbed from the bed and disappeared into the bathroom.

"Take your mind off your dick and tell me what the fuck was so important that you had to intrude on my pleasure time, Sidney," Prince Brown barked at his lieutenant.

"Willie Jackson is still alive and John Matthew bit the dust."

"Well spit in my ass and clear my brain!" Prince said. "That Jackson has my nerves on edge. Shit! Mr. Wright is not going to like this. Hell, we will burn the Silver Dollar tonight. At least that may give the boss some satisfaction."

"Sidney, you and Charles Lloyd, take Carlos Ward and Jim Clarke and get the fucking job done or your ugly mug won't be on planet earth breathing the same air like me, dig?"

"Yes, boss, we'll torch the club tonight; but boss, can I ask a favor of you?"

"No need to, yes you may fuck the whore, but on one condition."

"Name it, boss."

"I get to watch as you screw the hell out of her."

"Your wish is my command," Sidney said, dropping his trousers; to Prince's surprise Sidney had him by an inch and a half, so when Carla exited the bathroom, her eyes widened when she saw the length of Sidney's swollen penis, and now her tortured mind braced for the episode to follow.

"Do I have to, Mr. Brown? That monster is going to damage me. My pussy is on fire now from our encounter."

"He has my blessing and he promised to be gentle," Prince said with a smile.

The excitement was too much for Carla. She fainted and Sidney finished his ride uncontested, and, threw some water on her, which brought her back from her state of shock.

"Well done, Sidney," Prince Brown said. "Now go do what I'm paying you to do."

Chapter 23

M y sixth sense was sending me hot signals—which I couldn't make sense of. But there was a feeling that something might happen soon, and based on what Charles Lloyd had told us about Jason's destructive plan for the Silver Dollar, I now believed that the burning down of the club might be realized before tomorrow arrived.

When I left CID headquarters, I went to the Silver Dollar and told Martha to close at eleven tonight and take the important documents and float home with her.

"Are you expecting trouble, sir?" Martha asked before putting down her plate of chicken wings with a worried look on her face.

"I don't want you to worry, Martha. Just think of it as a precautionary exercise," I said coaxingly and saw a lovely smile light her face.

"Read you loud and clear, boss," she said, then picked her plate up and polished off the rest of the wings.

"Good girl, now don't make things look too obvious. You know how sentimental we all are when it comes to the Silver Dollar."

"I'll do things as normally as possible, boss."

"That's my gal."

I drank a stinger while sitting at the bar and took a second one for the road. Time was moving swiftly, and the sun had started its descent in the west to close out another day.

Everything was back to normal in my neighborhood, with the exception of a peeper named Mary Clare who lived in the apartment across the street from me, and I believe it was her who had summoned the police. Bless her peeping heart.

My telephone cried out and I picked it up.

"Jackson speaking, how may I be of service?"

"Johnson here, Willie. I'm coming over."

"I'll be awaiting your arrival, Serge," I said, then drank the rest of the stinger.

Jason Wright exited his bathroom in a velvet robe and looked at the three foxy ladies lying in their birthday suits sprawled over his king-sized bed. There was a mixed nationality at his disposal, all in their mid-twenties.

After dropping his robe, Jason and his bevy of beauties started to party with champagne and caviar. There was cocaine and marijuana on a side table for those who wanted to indulge in the drug scene.

After having his satisfaction met, Jason was brought up to date by Prince Brown, whom he joined in the living room.

"What's that you just said, Brown, that Jackson is still alive?"

"Yesss, sir, Mr Wright, but, his club will be burnt down at midnight. My men have their instructions and as we speak, they are putting their plans into action."

"Brown, you have been with me for a long time, and have never let me down before, but now you are starting to fuck up. I want Willie and his whore six feet under," Jason said as his complexion turned beet red. He got up abruptly from his chair and started pacing the floor.

"Yes, sir, but have you changed your mind? I thought you wanted to stuff his balls down his fuckin' throat, and by the way, information received is that whore wife of his has left the island."

"What was that about Joyce?" Jason asked as he came to a standstill.

"She's not on the island, sir," Prince said, stepping back as he cowered himself, afraid Jason might take a swing at him.

Sgt. Johnson and Detective Constable Moss pulled up in front of Jason's mansion and climbed out of the squad car. Their faces were not smiling, but their eyes said that they had had enough of the bullshit and it was high time that Jason and his men were given a one-way ticket to hell. I liked what I read and it was correct.

"We have the Silver Dollar covered, so when the suckers make their move, we'll slap cuffs on them," Johnson stated, and his eyes began to smile because his gut feeling was telling him that justice was soon to be served.

"Now let's go, I believe the big fishes are in the lake," Johnson said as he waved a folded paper in his hand, then went on to say, "I have a warrant for the arrest of Jason Wright and Prince Brown for the killing of Johnny Russell, Betty Wright, Elizabeth Culmer, and Sammy Strachan, and also for breathing God's clean air."

Jason's mansion situated on Halifax Streetwas dimly lit as Johnson and I advanced to the front door while Moss took the side entrance. In the distance, a dog began to howl as it looked at the full moon which was slowly climbing the heavens like a ghostly galleon amidst the rain clouds in the southern sky.

It was pure luck: no guards and both doors were unlocked. Jason and Prince were still in the living room when we entered. I could have sworn I heard Prince brokewind when he saw me with the gun in my hand.

"I have an arrest warrant for both of you," Johnson said, waving the paper at them.

"Go to hell, cop," Jason said, reaching for the gun on the sofa while Prince pulled his from his waistband. My bullet caught Prince in his chest as Jason retrieved his weapon and fired off a round, hitting me in the left shoulder as Johnson sent two slugs to Jason's chest just as his men came running down the stairs, bareback and guns in hand.

"Hold it, sucker!" Moss shouted. "Drop those weapons or get your asses blown to kingdom come!"

EPILOGUE

Carlos Ward, Sidney Hawkins, and Jim Clarke were taken into custody. Somehow Charles Lloyd was nowhere in sight when the officers swooped down on them as they began to throw gasoline on the Silver Dollar.

Joyce, Kathy, and Linda returned back to New Providence in time to celebrate our victory we had over Jason Wright and his minion Prince Brown, who were welcomed home by Satan.

Sgt. Johnson was promoted to Inspector and Moss went to the rank of Corporal.

Martha and the crew returned to work and business was as usual.

Carla Sweeting went out of her mind after two more of Prince Brown's boys pulled train on her after a cocaine binge, while the women at Jason's mansion were given a stiff warning and told to be of good behavior.

I received a call from Charles Lloyd thanking me for my accomplishment in ridding society of Jason Wright and Prince Brown. I thanked him for his help and he promised not to be a stranger at the Silver Dollar. I wondered if that would be good for business. I then said a prayer for Elizabeth Culmer because I didn't believe she was a bad person.

Maybe down the road somewhere she got sidetracked. But when she tried to make amends to society, her life was taken away from her. I believe her soul is resting in peace because that night at Thatch Palm and Bamboo Boulevard, I truly believed it was her voice I had heard whispering that she was alright now.

Last but not least, I turned to my naked wife and told her our honeymoon had just begun.

CPSIA information can be obtained
at www.ICGtesting.com
Printed in the USA
LVOW11s0618250417
532034LV00001B/3/P